The Rebound Effect

by

Linda Griffin

The Rebound Effect

Cover Art by *Abigail Owen*

The Wild Rose Press, Inc.
PO Box 708
Adams Basin, NY 14410-0708
Visit us at www.thewildrosepress.com

Publishing History
First Crimson Rose Edition, 2019
Print ISBN 978-1-5092-2659-7
Digital ISBN 978-1-5092-2660-3

Published in the United States of America

From the beginning this had been more sensuous than sexual, but now it was getting more personal by the minute. His hands were on her breasts, at first through the fabric and then underneath, stroking and cradling. She was neither frightened nor aroused, but he was very definitely making her feel something strong and deep. She held her breath, and he said, "Relax," again. He finally moved on, his hands warm on her bare midriff and her belly, down inside her shorts. Teresa moaned softly.

Draw a line, she told herself, but she didn't stop him. She was being manipulated, but she liked what he was doing. He moved on to her upper thighs, deeply kneading muscles that were a little tired from the beach, and on down her legs, with briefer attention to her feet this time, and back up the insides of her calves and thighs. One hand slipped between her legs. It was both an unpressured, natural continuation of the ritual and very deeply arousing.

She opened her eyes and looked into his. "This is supposed to relax me?" she asked.

"Yes." His hands were still now.

"This is supposed to make me trust you?" The thing was, she really wanted to trust him.

"Yes. Are you relaxed? Are you ready to go to sleep? Do you want me to kiss you good night and get in the other bed?"

Praise for Linda Griffin and *SEVENTEEN DAYS*

"*SEVENTEEN DAYS* was great! I couldn't put it down. The characters were well-developed and the dialogue was natural…The murder made the plot more exciting than that of a run-of-the-mill romance, but it didn't get in the way of the developing romance."

~Evelyn Kooperman, Author

~*~

"It was engaging enough to prevent me from putting the book down till I finished."

~Prospero 360, Online Book Club

~*~

"*SEVENTEEN DAYS* quickly develops into a pleasant, nicely paced story."

~Maggie Faria, InD'tale Magazine

Dedication

To Dick and Jane,
who first ignited my passion for the written word

Acknowledgments

Thanks are owed to my wonderful editor Nan Swanson for seeing past the pitfalls in the story and helping me make it better, to Martin L.A. Sternberg for the sign language dictionary, and to Edward Bulwer-Lytton for the dark and stormy night.

Chapter 1

Apple orchards stretched from end to end in Cougar Valley, but the soft earth along Big Devil Creek was where the bodies were buried. The creek—swollen to the size of a river since the Killwater Dam failed—was the boundary between the tiny town of Cougar and the unincorporated area beyond, and a lot of interested observers were gathered behind the yellow crime-scene tape on that crisp early fall morning.

The contingent was made up of five men in two official cars—two Powell City cops, Cougar's resident sheriff's deputy Hal Knight, a uniformed corrections officer, the prisoner in shackles—and a leashed German Shepherd trained as a cadaver dog. Everybody knew the story—Wade Linedecker had been convicted of the murders of two young women, but the bodies had never been found. Linedecker had refused to divulge their whereabouts on the grounds that it would amount to self-incrimination. Only when his first parole hearing was imminent had he decided to grant the victims' families the closure they longed for and lead authorities to the remains.

The back windows of the Rosey Lane Veterinary Clinic looked out over the creek, and the barking of two dogs boarding overnight alerted the staff to the presence of a strange canine in the vicinity. Dr. Veronica Saltzman and her assistant Teresa Lansing were among those who couldn't help gawking as the prisoner shuffled up and down the bank and pointed to several places. After a lengthy discussion, Linedecker pointed again before he was escorted back to one of the police cars. Deputy Knight began to dig in the first location, but the younger of the Powell City cops soon joined him. In spite of the cool weather, it was hot work, and both men took off their jackets.

Knight was in his forties and a little out of shape. The other one was younger, perhaps early thirties, and very fit. His hair was short and dark, which was about all they could tell from a distance. His eyes were hidden behind dark glasses, but the muscles were unmistakable. "He's hot," Dr. Saltzman said.

"You're married," Teresa reminded her.

"I can still look." They watched as the digging was suspended while the other Powell City officer squatted and sifted through the earth they had turned up. The prison guard joined the others, and their intense interest and discussion made it clear they had found something, although the dog was sniffing around a spot farther down the bank. The bell above the clinic door chimed as a customer entered. Veronica sighed. "Back to work," she said.

By the time they were finished with the diagnosis and treatment of a cocker spaniel's ear infection, the law enforcement group had filled what could only be a body bag and were digging in a second location. Cougar's local newspaper editor, John Trevor, had joined them, so full details would be in the next day's *Independent.*

As it turned out, Teresa would learn a little more of the story before the day was out.

****

The Cougar Bar & Grill was more than usually busy for a Thursday night, filled with the buzz of conversation and the inviting smells of sizzling meat and hot coffee, when Teresa came in with her six-year-old son Aiden. It was a regular event for them, a break in cooking routine for her and a treat for the boy. Alix English, the grill's proprietor, called out from behind the bar, "Oh, my God, here she comes! It's the terror of George Orwell High! And who is this handsome young man?"

"Hi, Alix," Teresa said. Aiden didn't respond, but he gave Alix the shy smile she could always win from him. Her seven-year-old daughter Sasha had better luck. She ran up and took his hand and led him to a booth in the corner, where they were soon busy with coloring books, Sasha chattering freely and occasionally using her limited American Sign Language vocabulary. Teresa didn't think he understood half of what she said, but it worked for them.

Teresa put in her order. Alix didn't need to ask what Aiden wanted; it was always the same. For him hot dogs and macaroni and cheese were the whole point of this exercise.

Alix nodded toward a table near the window. "VIPs," she said. Teresa turned her head just as one of the Powell City cops looked up. It was the younger, dark-haired one, and he gave her a look of undisguised interest. The correctional officer was not there—presumably he had returned Wade Linedecker to prison—but Deputy Knight was. The older city cop was flirting shamelessly with pretty blonde waitress Lacey Norman.

The dark-haired cop showed no interest in Lacey. He didn't look bored or contemptuous, just not interested. He got up and approached the counter, where Teresa was still talking to Alix. "Your better half's not with you tonight?" he asked. He had a pleasant baritone voice.

"What?" she said stupidly and then, recovering, "I'm not married."

"Oh, I thought you were," he said apologetically and smiled at her. He was disturbingly good-looking without his sunglasses, with penetrating brown eyes and just a trace of five o'clock shadow. He was tall, broad-shouldered, and very masculine, impressive if not intimidating. She liked his strong jaw line, and he had a nice smile, with just a hint of a dimple.

"Do I know you?" she asked. "I thought you were one of the Powell City officers."

"I am," he agreed, "but I live here. This is extra duty—they thought I could act as sort of a liaison. So the tall guy with the glasses—looks like a schoolteacher…?"

"Which he is," she said. "Or was, before he got fired. No, we were just dating."

"Fired?" he queried. "Why? Was he molesting little girls or something?"

"No, nothing like that, or at least I don't think so. He didn't want to talk about it."

"Want me to find out?" he asked.

"What?" He was in cop mode, but why? "No. I'm finished with him."

"I assume you dumped him," he said. "It couldn't have been the other way around."

She shrugged, even as she wondered why she was

discussing her romantic history with this stranger, who hadn't even offered his name. "It might as well be," she said. "When men cheat, isn't that one of the reasons? To end a relationship they want out of?"

"Is it? It sounds pretty cowardly. In your case, downright criminal. So you broke up recently? I don't want to seem too forward, but is it too soon for you to date?"

"I guess it depends on how you define date," she said.

"Well, could we maybe get together sometime?" he asked. "Dinner, someplace nice?"

"I don't even know you," she protested.

"Oh, I'm sorry. I'm Frank McAllister." He offered his hand, and Teresa, still bemused, took it. He had a firm handshake, a decent manicure, and no wedding ring.

"Teresa Lansing."

"I realize I'm a complete stranger to you, Teresa, but I feel like I know you. I've had my eye on you for a while, but I thought you were married. I'm glad I was wrong." He smiled again, looking into her eyes with flattering intensity. "He is your son, though, right?" He gestured toward the corner booth. His gaze lingered on Sasha and Aiden as the boy taught his friend a new sign. Frank McAllister didn't stop smiling, but a little line appeared between his eyes. He didn't say any of the usual things, which she appreciated.

"Yes, that's Aiden," she said neutrally.

Sasha's voice was clearly audible, and Frank said, "Little kids' voices sound like a joke, you know? Like a comic fooling around with falsetto."

"You don't have children," she deduced.

"No, and I guess I haven't been around them enough. So, what do you think? Could I…call you, or…" He had seemed pretty confident, but now a shade of doubt crept in. Teresa was still deciding what she should say when he said, "He's here."

"Who?"

"The guy you're not married to." He nodded toward the door, and Teresa turned to see Brett Devlin just coming in. She looked away before he could spot her, but she felt a certain satisfaction in thinking he might notice she was with an attractive man. She gave McAllister her phone number. She could always brush him off later. When she looked around again, Brett was gone—scared off? He knew she would be at the grill— she always was on Thursday evenings.

Aiden came back and tugged at her hand. He didn't look at McAllister, perhaps didn't even notice him. He signed quickly, "Mama, I need bathroom."

"Didn't I tell you to go before we left?" she asked, speaking and signing simultaneously. She didn't wait for an answer and took his hand. He was old enough to go into the grill's small men's room by himself, but she still insisted on checking to see if it was empty first. When she was satisfied, she returned to the counter and kept an eye on the door.

"He doesn't speak?" Frank McAllister asked.

"Yes, he does. He goes to speech therapy, but he's such a little perfectionist he rarely uses his voice in public."

"Have you thought about a cochlear implant?"

"I've thought about how expensive they are," she said. "It's about sixty thousand, maybe more, including the surgery and rehab, and my insurance won't cover it."

"What about his father? Is he in the picture?"

"No, not really. So you live in Cougar? I don't think I've seen you before."

"I've been here four months. I'm in the city so much, working, that it doesn't feel like home yet, but I like it. It seems like a nice place to settle down. Unusual name, Cougar. Has anybody seen one around here?"

"Yes, we've had sightings, and a farmer shot one last year. I haven't seen any, but you can guess what the high school football team is called."

"The Cougars. And why were you the terror of Orwell High?"

"You heard that? It's just a silly nickname Alix gave me—Teresa, Terror. I was a good girl!"

"I bet you were," he said. The tone of admiration in his voice was unmistakable, his smile very warm. "Were you a cheerleader?"

"Far from it." Was he for real? She wasn't remarkable in any way, so why this interest? He had thought she was married, after all. He seemed to be unaware of the charms of teen-aged Lacey Norman, which included big blue eyes and knockers to match. She always displayed them to their best advantage too, with lots of makeup and daringly low-cut blouses. Teresa was slender, twenty-eight, and dressed in jeans and a T-shirt that revealed nothing. "How long have you been a police officer?" she asked.

"Twelve years. I'm on the SWAT team, so this isn't my usual gig."

"SWAT? Wow! Aiden would be impressed. So you just came to help dig up bodies?"

"Mostly bones, actually—they'd been dead a long time. Thing is—it will be public knowledge tomorrow, so I might as well tell you—Linedecker confessed to the two murders he was convicted of, but we found three bodies."

"Wow!" she said again. Just then Lacey sashayed past with Aiden's hot dogs and macaroni and cheese in one hand and Teresa's quesadillas in the other, trailing a mix of cheap scent and hot spices. Teresa said, "Well..." and gestured toward the table where the boy now sat alone. Sasha had gone into the kitchen "to get in the way," as Alix would have it.

"I'll let you go," McAllister said. "I'll call you." He went back to his fellow officers.

"We-ell!" Alix said. "He works fast."

"It must be my sexy outfit."

Alix laughed. "What do you think?" she asked.

"Charming, but kind of cocky."

"Very high testosterone level. Look out, kiddo."

"You know me—Miss Cautious. He probably won't call anyway—he'll look around and find something better. Or easier," she added, with a glance at Lacey. She gave Alix a quick wave and hurried to join her son.

When she sat down in the booth, he signed, "Who that man?"

"Policeman," she said and signed, adding S-W-A-T in fingerspelling.

His eyes widened. "True?"

"Yes, really. Eat your salad."

"Too much green," he complained.

"Green is good for you."

"Why?"

"It just is. You want to grow up big and strong, don't you?"

Aiden's gaze went immediately to the table where the police officers were getting up to leave. She shouldn't have told him about SWAT—he was a little too prone to hero worship, and if McAllister was going to be around, it was best for him not to get attached too soon. It was one of the lessons she had learned with Brett.

****

Frank McAllister called the next morning. She didn't recognize the number and didn't answer until he started to leave a voicemail. "Sorry," she said briskly, "I'm at work and wasn't expecting—"

"I won't keep you," he said apologetically. "Where do you work?"

"The vet clinic—right above where you were digging."

"Oh, yeah—small white building with a blue roof? I don't want to take you away from your patients, but I wondered if we could have dinner tonight?"

"Oh, I don't think I can get a babysitter on such short notice." Not to mention that it was rude of him to assume she wouldn't be otherwise engaged.

"I'm sorry—I know I'm going a little bit fast here. Tomorrow, then?"

"Weekends are always tricky—teenagers have plans." Had she decided to brush him off or not? She didn't need to complicate her life any more right now, and he seemed like trouble—why, exactly? That was the point of a first date, wasn't it? To get to know each other well enough to judge whether it might be worth the trouble?

"Next week? If a weekday is better—"

"I couldn't stay out late," she hedged.

"Just dinner," he agreed.

She took a deep breath. "Monday would be okay, but I work until seven on Mondays."

"Do you know the perfect place?"

"What—you want me to choose?"

He laughed. "No, I mean that's what it's called: the Perfect Place. It's a nice restaurant in Powell City, very good food, and obviously the management isn't at all modest. It won't be busy Monday evenings, so—eight? I'd pick you up at seven-thirty?"

"I guess it would be all right," she said cautiously.

"Great! I'll make a reservation. Sorry about calling you at work."

"It's okay." She gave him the address.

"See you Monday." He hung up, and Teresa resumed cleaning and dressing the wounds of a battle-scarred tomcat. She tried not to think about what she might have gotten herself into.

At lunchtime, she called Alix and asked if she knew anything about a restaurant called the Perfect Place. "The perfect place for what is the question," her friend replied. She promptly Googled it, but found only a coffee shop in South Africa and a restaurant in Italy. "My advice is to dress up, but be a little standoffish. I'll call you with a 'babysitting emergency' at eight-thirty—you should know by then how it's going."

"What would I do without you?" Teresa asked.

Chapter 2

Teresa wished Alix was there Monday evening when she was trying to decide what to wear. Alix believed in dressing to dazzle, but she didn't want to be overdressed if the Perfect Place turned out to be casual. Frank had said "nice"—did he mean upscale, or just pleasant? If she wore something fancy, he would be disappointed when she later proved to be a T-shirt and jeans girl—but he had already seen her that way.

She chose her best outfit—a cream silk dress with long sleeves and a moderately low neckline. She added a silver locket and the silver-and-pearl earrings Brett had given her for Christmas. She put her hair up, with a few stray locks over her ears so it wouldn't look too severe. While she was fussing with it, Aiden brought her a handful of beads from one of his craft projects. "Pretty in your hair," he signed and for emphasis said, "Pretty," with a slight roll of the r.

"Thank you, sweetie," she said and kissed him as a reward for the good speech effort. She took a few of the beads and threaded them into her hair to humor him. She fully intended to take them out as soon as Alix and Sasha picked him up for the sleepover, but they actually looked very appropriate. He had even chosen the right colors—silver, white, black, and red.

The first thing Alix said was, "Oh, I like the beads."

Teresa patted Aiden's back. "My son is a fashion guru."

"That was your idea?" Alix asked him. "Smart as well as handsome!" She turned back to Teresa. "You look great," she said. "I hope he's worthy of it."

Aiden had been too excited about the sleepover to ask much about Teresa's plans, but now he inquired, "Mama go party?"

"No, just dinner. If you decide you don't want to stay with Sasha, tell Alix to call me and I'll pick you up. I won't stay out late."

"I won't call," he signed indignantly. "I not baby!"

"I know, I know, you're—"

"Six!" He said it aloud, nailing the tricky x sound.

She bent swiftly to kiss his forehead. "He doesn't let me get away with *anything*," she complained.

He and Sasha disappeared into his room to get his backpack, and Alix said, "Keep your wits about you, Terror. You look good enough to eat, but don't let him."

Teresa laughed. "He's not the big, bad wolf," she said.

"Don't be so sure," Alix advised. "Don't let him get you drunk or high. Keep an eye on your glass."

When Alix and the children were gone, she wavered a bit—maybe she was too dressed up. If he showed up in dungarees, she would die of embarrassment. But he had said "nice," and if it was jeans-friendly he should have said so. It would be a definite sign of incompatibility, and she could forget him and his nice smile.

She was contemplating lipstick shades when the doorbell rang. Frank McAllister's stock immediately went down—didn't he know any better than to be early when a woman was getting dolled up? She hurried to the door, flustered and annoyed—and it wasn't him.

Brett Devlin stood on her small porch. He looked nervous—and very neat, his shirt pressed, his hair combed, as if he was as anxious to make a good impression tonight as she was. He had one hand behind his back and didn't seem to know what to do with the other one. Exasperated, Teresa snapped, "Didn't I make myself clear?"

He raised his hand in a calming gesture. "Yes, you did—oh, Jesus, you're all dressed up. You're going out already?"

"It's none of your business what I do," she said curtly.

"Okay, okay—I was just surprised. I mean, you look really nice and everything. I just—"

"You're not welcome here, Brett. I told you I didn't want to see you again."

"Have a heart, Reesie. I said I was sorry." The misery in his voice hurt, but she steeled herself to maintain her righteous indignation.

"I'm not your Reesie anymore. I don't need you to say you're sorry. I need you to be sorry enough not to do any more damage."

"Damage…? Okay, obviously my timing stinks. I'll call first next time."

"There'd better not be a next time." She stepped back, ready to close the door.

"Wait, wait," he said, "I found this—" He brought his hand out from behind his back and held up a shopping bag with a long box sticking out the top. According to the lettering on the end she could see, it contained a remote-controlled helicopter.

"You can't buy your way back into my favor. You hurt me, and you hurt Aiden. It's a good thing he isn't here—"

"I know; I saw him with Alix. Please, I want him to have it. You don't have to tell him it's from me. I saw it, and I knew he'd love it."

"It's too old for him. He's six, not eight." She tapped the box where it said *Ages 8-up*.

"Oh, come on, those are guidelines. He's a smart kid, and he's almost seven. I had stuff like this when I was six."

"They didn't make stuff like this when you were six. It's sophisticated electronics. You have to leave."

"Please, Teresa. I made a mistake, but—"

"I don't have time for this." She closed the door in his face and didn't watch to see if he left. She went back to the bathroom and forced herself to take a few deep breaths. There was no point in doing this if she couldn't relax and enjoy herself.

She glanced out the front window at exactly seven-thirty, and Frank was getting out of his car—a new, dark blue Acura SUV, which probably cost more than her annual salary. SWAT officers made good money—or he was willing to go into debt for a fancy car. He got points for punctuality, anyway. He wasn't wearing jeans, but slacks, jacket, and tie. He looked smart, but not too formal, so her dress should pass muster.

She waited for him to ring the doorbell and counted to three before she answered it. High school tricks—she was out of practice. He smiled as soon as he saw her. "Hi, Teresa. Wow, you look great."

"Not so bad yourself," she said. "I wasn't sure—

I'm more of a jeans-type girl."

"Yeah, I figured you were, but you cleaned up real nice." He grinned. "This is a cute little house—is it yours?"

"It's a rental," she said. "I don't make a lot of money. 'Cute' is an overstatement, but at least the roof doesn't leak." She locked the door—she didn't usually bother, but he was a cop and might think it was stupid not to—and preceded him down the walkway to his car.

"You're a veterinarian?" he asked.

"No, I'm only an assistant. I'd like to be, but I couldn't afford to finish college." He opened the car door for her. "Nice car," she said.

He nodded toward the old pickup in the driveway. "That your ride?"

"Yes. It's not pretty, but it runs."

"That's the important thing." He made sure her skirt was clear, closed the door, and went around to the driver's side. The interior of the Acura was even more impressive, with luxurious upholstery, comfortable seats, and a dashboard full of high-tech gadgetry. It still had traces of new-car smell.

"I guess the PCPD pays well," she said.

"I can't complain," he said, "and I've made some good investments. Of course, we all took a hit when the economy tanked."

"I don't know anything about investments," she said. "Putting my paycheck in the bank is as daring as I get."

He laughed and started the car. "It's a crime how little savings accounts pay these days," he said. "You said the boy's father—"

"We're divorced," she said.

"Child support?"

"No. It's a long story. Actually, it's not a very original story—high school sweethearts, got married too young, grew apart. And he blamed me—not because Aiden was deaf, but because he wasn't diagnosed sooner. He thought we overlooked early signs because I was too protective. I won't say any more—nothing's worse than listening to a woman bitch about her ex. Have you ever been married? You don't live with your mother, do you?"

He laughed. "No, I'm not *that* guy. Yes, I was married once."

"What happened?" she asked casually, but when he didn't answer right away, she added, "None of my business."

"Well, Teresa," he said, "She up and died on me."

"Oh, I'm sorry!"

"I'm sorry too; I didn't mean to sound flippant. It's just—you don't stop minding, but you stop having to be dramatic about it. It is what it is."

"Anyway, I'm sorry. I guess I'm lucky. I haven't lost anybody yet."

"Do your folks live here?"

"In the city now. The land I grew up on is leased to an apple grower."

"Will you inherit it?"

"Probably not. More likely it will be sold to pay their debts."

"Are you close to them—your parents?"

"Not as close as I'd like to be. They love Aiden, and we do Christmas and so on, but I think they're disappointed in me. They liked Gene, my husband, and Brett too. They're starting to think I can't hold on to a decent guy."

"Or maybe they can't hold on to you," he said. "You haven't found the right one yet, that's all. Fair warning, Teresa: I'm the tenacious kind."

"I stand warned. It's not always a good thing, though." She hadn't meant to say anything, but he was surprisingly easy to talk to. "Brett—the guy I was dating—showed up at my door a few minutes before you did."

Frank frowned. "If he's harassing you, you could get a restraining order."

"I don't need one. It's not like that. Good thing, because if I did need one, it would be just a piece of paper."

"I know what you mean," he said. "A lot of my work begins with a domestic violence call."

"Really? Not hostages and bank robberies?"

"Not usually. Mostly drunks with weapons, threatening family members or the neighbors. Or we serve high-risk warrants, stuff like that."

"Or dig up bodies," she said.

He laughed. "And you were up on the hill watching me sweat? Maybe I wasn't the only one who liked what I saw."

"My boss thought you were hot, anyway. You said before you'd had your eye on me—where did you see me?"

"Different places, always with the schoolteacher."

"Actually, he drives a truck for an orchard now."

"What did he want today?"

"He had something for Aiden, but I didn't take it."

"Was it serious with you two?"

"Yes. I thought so, anyway. We talked about

getting married, about him adopting Aiden. Cheating wasn't the worst thing he did. He got close to Aiden—they were buddies—and then he betrayed us. Aiden isn't over it yet."

"Are you?"

She shrugged. "I'm tough," she said, "and I'm not six and isolated by deafness."

"So you're not one of those who think deaf kids aren't broken and don't need to be fixed?"

"Well, he's not broken, but he is limited."

"You don't agree with the people who say learning to speak is an insult to Deaf culture?"

"ASL *is* a language and has its own literature—poetry and plays—and I guess you can build a culture on that, but I don't see anything wrong with being bilingual. It's a hearing world, especially in a small town where he won't meet a lot of other deaf kids. I guess it's different in cities where they have special schools and clubs and support groups."

"Have you thought about moving to a city?"

"I've even tried it, but Cougar is home."

"Good for you. You said you didn't finish college, but I can tell from the way you talk you're more educated than most of the folks around here."

"Oh, really? So it was my brain you were interested in?"

He grinned. "Yes, of course."

Chapter 3

The exterior of the Perfect Place was more modest than its name, a simple square building with the name in block capitals above tall windows. It had no valet parking, and Frank let Teresa out at the front door because "I wouldn't want you to walk too far in those shoes." She didn't think he had even glanced at her shoes, which were low-heeled pumps, but she was glad to have a few minutes to catch her breath and think about the conversation so far. He seemed very interested in her and had said little about himself. She should have asked when his wife died. He might be out of practice too.

He had asked a lot of questions about finances—did she own her house, the pickup, get child support, would she inherit the family farm. He had mentioned investments and the low interest rates on savings. Maybe he would try to involve her in some kind of pyramid scheme. It wouldn't matter—she didn't have anything to invest.

Before she could come to any conclusions, he was back and opened the door for her. The interior was welcoming, with soft lighting, brick, wood paneling, exposed overhead beams, and lush carpet. Frank gave his name at the desk, and they were immediately conducted to a table with a white cloth, real silverware, and very comfortable chairs. Teresa was a little intimidated and looked around to make sure the other diners weren't in formal wear. They weren't.

The waitress, Rachel, wore a tie. She was a pretty brunette, but Frank didn't seem to notice. She offered them menus, poured ice water, and asked if they would like wine. Teresa shook her head, and Frank followed her lead. When the waitress was out of hearing, he asked, "Are you in AA or something?"

"No. I stopped drinking when I was pregnant and never found a good time to start again. It's not like I was a big drinker before. A glass of wine with dinner would be fine, but I think I'd better keep my wits about me tonight."

"You think I'm dangerous?" he asked, smiling. "I'm flattered."

She directed her attention to the menu. The prices made her a little anxious, but she assumed he could afford it. The children's menu included macaroni and cheese, which made her think of Aiden and relax a little.

"I can recommend the New York steak and the ribs," Frank said. "I haven't tried anything else, but I'm sure they're good too."

She reminded herself this was a rare occasion deserving of the suspension of diet rules and chose the lobster linguini. Rachel brought warm bread and took their orders. Conversation had been easy in the car, but now Teresa had to look into those intense brown eyes, and she couldn't think of a thing to say.

"Let's see," he said. "What am I supposed to ask on a first date? Not your sign—favorite color?"

"Blue."

"Me too. I knew we'd have something in common.

Pet peeve?"

She didn't hesitate. "People who take driving too casually. It's a very dangerous occupation, requiring your undivided attention."

"Hard to do with kids in the car, though," he suggested.

"Yes, but it's the kids in the car who make it most necessary."

"I can tell you're a good mother," he said. "It's too bad you have to work. I'm sure stay-at-home moms give kids the best start, but it takes a certain kind of woman to pull it off these days."

"Yeah," she said. "A rich one."

"Or one who's getting the support she deserves. Your ex-husband—"

She shook her head. "I don't want to talk about him."

"Okay, let's try another one. What do you want out of life?"

She considered. "For my son to grow up happy and healthy. It's my turn. What's *your* pet peeve?"

"Men who don't appreciate a woman like you." His bold look, more than the words, made Teresa blush. He was so emphatically male he made slender, bespectacled Brett look like a boy. Maybe that was the problem—Brett wasn't mature yet. "Sorry, I didn't mean to make you uncomfortable," he said. "Okay, here's one—movie trailers that tell too much."

That led to a lively discussion—most egregious previews, favorite trailers, movies they had both seen or wanted to. It continued even after dinner was served, and somewhere along the line it came to be assumed they would spend their second date in a movie theater.

The food looked and smelled wonderful. Teresa told herself she'd better enjoy every bite. She wasn't likely to continue dating someone who took this sort of thing for granted, so it was a one-time opportunity. She wasn't sure whether to cut the pasta or twirl it like spaghetti and wished she had chosen a less complicated dish, but Frank had ordered the same entrée, and she could follow his lead. He cut the pasta with his fork, and she breathed a secret sigh of relief. The lobster was fresh and tender, the linguini buttery, the wine sauce perfect.

"Like it?" he asked when her mouth was full, and she could only nod enthusiastically. He laughed and took another bite. "Me too—this might be my new favorite. Don't forget to save room for dessert, though."

"Oh, no," she said. The generous serving of linguini was more than she would be able—or dare—to eat. Would it be tacky to ask for a doggie bag in a place like this? Aiden would love it, even reheated in the microwave. He wouldn't care about the creamy wine sauce or distinguish lobster from tuna, but noodles were noodles.

"Oh, yes," Frank said. "They have a triple chocolate tiramisu you can't resist."

"Triple—Mr. McAllister, you're trying to seduce me… Aren't you?"

"Yes," he answered, smiling, "but I'm in no hurry. I have a feeling you're worth waiting for." He said it lightly, with laughter, a joking response to her *The Graduate* reference, but also very possibly serious.

She didn't know how to respond or remember where they had left the film discussion and could only continue to enjoy the linguini with appropriate murmurs of approval. She was rescued by the chime of her cell phone. "Excuse me, I need to take this," she said apologetically. Frank didn't look annoyed, but she noticed a chilly look from another diner.

It was Alix, of course. "Major babysitting disaster!" she announced, but with laughter in her voice. "How's it going, kiddo?"

"Fine," Teresa said comfortably. "I'll talk to you later."

"Yeah?" Alix said eagerly. "Is he behaving himself?"

"Sort of," she said. "The food is fantastic. Bye!" She hung up. "I'm sorry," she said. "I know it's rude, but—"

"You're a mother," he said, nodding. "I left mine on too, because I'm always on call. We both have jobs that don't respect the clock."

"It was Alix," she confessed. "She called with an invented emergency in case I needed to make a quick exit."

"Women really do that?" he asked. "Not just in the movies?"

"Yes—men don't?"

"Not that I know of. Have you ever taken advantage of it? Left the guy in the lurch, I mean?"

"Oh, it sounds terrible when you say it like that. No—or once, in high school. The boy had a few beers with his buddies before our date, and he was loud and obnoxious and all hands. My friend, who was at the same party, called me from the bathroom, and I told him my dog had been hit by a car."

"At least you were original. You told me the trick—does that mean you trust me?"

"Apparently. Are you trustworthy?"

"No," he said, laughing. "Not where you're concerned."

"Do you say things like that to all your dates, or was that your George Clooney impression?"

"It depends."

"On what?"

"How you feel about George Clooney."

"Everybody loves George Clooney."

"Okay, here's one—favorite Clooney role?"

"*Good Night and Good Luck.*"

"Really? I knew you were smart, Teresa. What about the one he won the Oscar for?"

"*Syriana?* I guess I didn't get it."

"Well, you wouldn't want to be *too* smart," he said. "It was depressing anyway. Here's one I bet you didn't see: *Men Who Stare at Goats.*"

"Yes, I did. Bizarre!"

"And it was a true story. Did you see *Burn After Reading?*"

By the time they were done with the movies, they were ready for dessert, and she realized she still didn't know anything about him beyond his film preferences. "Tell me about your job," she urged. "Did you work today?"

"Yes. It wasn't very interesting, I'm afraid. The highlight of the day was multiple calls about shots being fired inside a house, but it was a bust—nobody there, no guns, no signs of violence."

"It could still have been a crime scene."

"Possibly, but it's somebody else's headache."

"Would you want to be a detective?"

"I started out wanting to go that route, but I guess

I'm a little bit of an adrenaline junkie. I like my job."

"Does it pay well?" Now she was the one asking financial questions.

"I make eighty-eight thou," he said casually.

Teresa could barely suppress a gasp. "It's three times what I make," she told him. It was more than she and Brett had earned together.

"Then you're underpaid, or I'm overpaid. Probably both."

The waitress returned and asked what else she could bring them. "Could we have two boxes?" Frank asked. He had eaten about half of his linguini, and Teresa only a third of hers.

"Certainly, sir. Would you like to see a dessert menu?"

"That won't be necessary. We'll have the tiramisu and coffee."

"Decaf for me," Teresa said. She should have said no to the dessert too, but reminded herself this was not going to happen again.

"Wait 'til you taste this," he said when Rachel was gone. "Have you ever had *Zuppa Inglese*?"

"I've never even heard of it," she confessed. "I'm afraid I'm more of a cheeseburger-and-fries girl. This was wonderful, but I wouldn't want to do it every week. I hope you were just trying to impress me..."

"Did I?"

"Yes, but I'm also a little intimidated. I don't think I can keep up with you. Maybe you should look for somebody more compatible."

He shook his head. "We like the same kind of movies, though, right?"

"It seems like it."

"Okay, next week we'll see a movie and save places like this for special occasions. This was one, for me, anyway."

"Oh, Frank, it was very special. Thank you. I'm a little embarrassed because you spent so much money on me, and I probably sound ungrateful."

"Money doesn't mean anything to me," he said dismissively.

"Only because you have enough. It's very important to people like me."

"I hope that will change," he said. "Anyway, it was the first time you used my first name, so that's a plus."

Rachel returned with a cart and poured the coffee. The tiramisu came in generous portions, sprinkled with cocoa powder, drizzled with chocolate sauce, and with a chocolate wafer stuck in the top of each piece. "Oh, my God," Teresa said. "You *are* trying to seduce me."

Rachel laughed. "It's worth it," she said and whisked the cart away again.

Teresa took a cautious bite, and it melted in her mouth. "This is fantastic," she said. "What is *Zuppa…?*"

"*Zuppa Inglese.* It's similar, but dipped in this great red liqueur instead of coffee. It may have been the original version."

"It couldn't be better than this." She promised herself she wouldn't eat it all and tried to take very small bites.

Frank sampled his, but it didn't have his full attention. "So you're telling me you're trying to raise your boy on less than thirty—"

"It's easier in Cougar than it would be somewhere else."

"Still. Did Devlin help?"

"Yes…I didn't tell you his last name, did I?"

He shrugged. "I asked around."

"Don't," she said sharply. "It's over."

"Not if he's still coming around."

"He isn't. Today was the last time. I told him how I felt."

"Okay. Would you let me help you?"

"No, of course not!" He was spoiling the tiramisu for her.

"I don't mean to cross a line here," he said soothingly. "I only want to help."

"Thank you. I'll manage."

"I understand you don't want to be obligated, but it would be so easy for me—"

She shook her head. "Money is never easy. Did you think I'd be easy because—?"

"No, Teresa," he said firmly. "I won't pretend I didn't think about taking you to bed the first time I saw you, but right now I want to get to know you. What I really need is somebody to go to the movies with."

She took a deep breath. "I'm sorry. It's just hard to trust anybody right now. I knew Brett for years, and I never would have believed he was the kind to…do what he did."

"Do you think I am?" he asked.

"Yes," she said and laughed in spite of herself, a shaky laugh, but genuine, and he smiled in response.

"I figure you can react one of two ways after a betrayal," he said. "Decide not to trust anybody, or figure you can trust a stranger as easily as the guy next door."

Distracted, she said, "This is *so* good!"

****

It was dark and a bit chilly when they left the restaurant, and Frank suggested Teresa wait inside while he got the car. "I'll go with you," she said. "I need to walk off all those calories." He took her hand very casually—the first time he had touched her since their brief handshake on meeting. "If I ate like this all the time, I'd get fat," she said.

"It wouldn't hurt you to put a little meat on your bones," he said.

"You sound like my mother," she said. "I'm the ideal weight for my height."

"I just meant you don't have to try to be some perfect stereotype fashion model or something. I appreciate your getting all dolled up for me tonight, but you don't have to."

"It was fun for a change," she said.

"Good." He squeezed her hand. The car was close by, and he opened her door for her.

She hadn't been in the city at night for a long time, and the traffic and lights were strangely bright and chaotic. She was glad when they turned off the main highway and onto the familiar roads of Cougar. Even in the dark she knew every inch of it.

As he pulled up in front of her house, Frank asked, "Would you like me to drive the babysitter home?"

"Actually, Aiden is at Alix's tonight. The grill is closed on Mondays." She didn't need to tell him everything, but somehow the truth flowed naturally in his presence.

"So could I come in for a few minutes?" he asked. "Just to see the house?"

She shook her head. "Not tonight. I do have to

make it an early night. I promised to pick Aiden and Sasha up in the morning and make pancakes for them before school."

He got out and came around to open her door. "Your friend Alix is a single mom too?" he asked.

"Her husband was killed in Afghanistan."

"Oh, that's rough," he said sympathetically. He followed her up the stairs to her door. She thought he would ask again to come in, but he said nothing while she dug out her key.

"Thank you, Frank. I had a very good time."

"Me too," he said. He handed her both boxes of leftovers and bent his head to kiss her. It was not a polite first-date kiss. She liked it, but afterward she took a step back, braced for something—she didn't know what. Her heart was beating a little too fast.

"Sorry," he murmured. "I knew I was going to have trouble with you."

"Trouble?"

"Controlling myself." He stepped back too, smiling. "Good night, Teresa. I'll call you about a movie."

"Good night, Frank."

Chapter 4

When Teresa drove up in front of Alix's white clapboard ranch house, her son came running out the front door. "Mama!" He yanked on the door handle before she could unlock it, and when she did he was immediately half on top of her, grinning into her face and signing furiously. It was too much for her to sort out, but she gathered he had had a good time.

"Slow down," she cautioned and gave him a resounding kiss.

Only one thing was bothering him. "Sasha say devil live in Big Devil River."

"She's teasing you, sweetie. Devils are only in stories."

"Except the human ones," Alix called from the porch. To Aiden she signed, "Sasha big liar!" with exaggerated movements and a laughing expression.

Teresa gave the boy back the beads she had worn in her hair. "Thank you. I felt so pretty last night!" She got out of the car, and he hung onto her hand, pulling her toward the house.

"Well?" Alix asked. "How was your big date?"

"It was fine."

"Fine? Cover your ears, Aiden," she joked. "Give me details, girl."

"The food was good. The restaurant was expensive, but not scary. He was easy to talk to. He didn't talk

30

about himself much. I can't figure him out."

"How so?"

"Is he for real? What does he see in me?"

"Well, you're not entirely repulsive most of the time, you know."

"If it's not real, what does he want?"

"Did he ask you for money?"

"Get real. I don't have any, and he has plenty."

"Sex?" Alix suggested.

"Lacey Norman would be easier."

"Some men prefer your type—you know, marginally intelligent."

"Yeah, right. My parents taught me if something seems too good to be true, it probably is."

"Uh-huh. And did they teach you every rule has exceptions?"

"Yeah, maybe. He seems too smooth to be real, and then he'll say something that seems genuine."

"Like you would know, after Brett. So what are you going to do about it?"

Teresa shrugged. "Go to the movies with him, I guess. See how it goes."

"Oh, good. Sounds like high school." Alix opened the screen door and yelled, "Sasha! Get your cute little ass out here!"

Sasha appeared almost at once, carrying Aiden's backpack. She signed to him, "Mama say A-S-S," and they both giggled.

"Good work," Teresa said to Alix.

She shrugged. "At least our kids can spell."

****

Frank called at ten-thirty. "I'm sorry; I got you at work again, didn't I?"

Teresa held the phone against her shoulder while she cleaned the teeth of a very patient collie. "Yes," she said. "Good boy! Sorry, that wasn't meant for you. I'm almost finished with…" She dropped the phone, scrambled to retrieve it, and was too flustered to think of anything to say except, "Sorry," again. She scratched the collie's ears.

"Obviously you're busy. I'm on a break, but I wanted to say thank you for last night, and when can I see you again? When is good to take in a movie?"

She took a deep breath. "To be perfectly honest, I haven't seen a movie in a theater in years. Aiden can't read the captions fast enough yet, and he only likes animation anyway."

"You're definitely overdue, then. Would Saturday night work? Maybe grab a bite to eat after? No fancy restaurants, I promise."

"I'll see if I can get my regular sitter. Can I call you back?"

"Sure," he said warmly. "Any time." After she hung up she had to fan herself. Was it dropping the phone or something in his voice?

When Veronica came in, she said, "What's the matter? You look a little pink." She put her hand on Teresa's forehead. "No fever."

"I'm fine," Teresa assured her, laughing. "I think I have a crush on a hot guy."

"Good for you. I hope this one doesn't break your heart."

****

She was able to line up Chelsea Ryan, the one teenage girl she was willing to trust with Aiden, for Saturday night, and Frank intended to pick her up at six o'clock, but a little after five he called to cancel. "I have to work," he said. "I'll call you later," and he hung up.

It seemed rude, abrupt, and she didn't know him well enough to guess if it was uncharacteristic. She reminded herself of what he did for a living, but she was still annoyed. Canceling the babysitter at the last minute was likely to make it harder to get her the next time, but mostly she was childishly disappointed at the last-minute cancellation of an outing she was looking forward to.

Only when Aiden was in bed and she turned on the ten o'clock news did she understand—a SWAT standoff was underway in Powell City, and two people had been shot. She couldn't recognize Frank in the brief images of the officers at the scene, but they were all alike in their helmets and body armor, carrying heavy weapons and looking much like combat soldiers.

She didn't like the feeling he might be in danger. Did she want to date somebody for whom this kind of scenario was routine? The newscaster hadn't said whether the two gunshot victims were officers or civilians. She resisted the temptation to stay up in hope of updates, but she didn't sleep well.

Frank called at eight a.m. "I'm really sorry," he said. "I don't know if you heard—"

"Yes. I saw the news. It's over?"

"Yes, the perp killed himself. I didn't want to wake you up or I would have called when it ended. You weren't still asleep, were you?"

"No, no, we're having breakfast."

"Could I maybe come by later? I need a couple more hours sleep, but I'd like to see you, and I want to meet your boy."

"It's too early for that," she said. "He still asks for Brett. It's too soon to introduce somebody else. And we have church and Sunday school, and I have a lot—"

"Okay, I get the message. Tonight, though?" She felt a little crowded by his persistence, but she had been looking forward to an adult movie outing. Her hesitation wasn't lost on him. "Am I pushing too hard?" he asked.

"No, it's all right. I'll see if I can get the sitter again."

****

Chelsea was nice about it—she had gone out with friends the night before, so she still had homework to do, and she needed the money. Aiden didn't want Teresa to go out again, but he would be fine with Chelsea. He came to lean against her, shortly before Frank was due, and signed, "I will miss you, Mama." He repeated, "Miss you," in a mournful voice.

"I'll miss you too, sweetie. Good speech. Very expressive." She hugged him close to her side.

"Can I go to movie?"

"You wouldn't like it. It's a boring grownup movie. Talk, talk, talk. And Chelsea will be sad if you don't stay and play with her."

He glanced at Chelsea, who was setting up the Quirkle game on the kitchen table. " 'kay," he said and went to join her.

Teresa reminded Chelsea of Aiden's bedtime and her cell phone number posted on the refrigerator. "He's eaten," she said, "but there are leftovers if you get hungry," and then she hurried to run a comb through her hair before Frank arrived. She had deliberately dressed down in contrast to her dinner-date outfit—dark jeans, a pullover sweater, sneakers, and no makeup except lipstick and a touch of eye shadow. If he didn't like her this way, he didn't like *her*.

Apparently he did—he smiled when he saw her. He wore jeans too, with a long-sleeved blue shirt. "No bullet holes," she commented.

He laughed. "No, there wasn't much danger of that."

"But two people were shot?"

"Nobody died," he assured her. "Except the shooter."

"I hate guns," she said with feeling.

"They do cause a lot of trouble," he agreed. "This dude had a semi-automatic rifle. You know this movie has guns in it?" He opened the car door for her.

"Yes," she said. "But it's Tom Hanks."

On the drive in to the Cineplex 16 in Powell City, he told her a little more about the standoff. The victims, a man and a woman, were hospitalized but in good condition. "It was tense, but not too dangerous. Just more overtime pay for me." She imagined he was downplaying the danger for her sake, but he was certainly matter-of-fact about it.

They talked about movies too, and soon she was so inexplicably comfortable with him she found herself telling him about her failed marriage. "Sorry," she said. "Whining about my ex again."

"No, no," he said. "I want to know everything about you. Obviously, it's his loss, but I guess it's hard on a man to realize his son isn't perfect."

"I still think he's perfect!" Teresa said, bristling.

"I'm sure you do. Mother love—nothing like it. It's

harder for us mere mortals."

"You haven't said anything about your family. Do they live around here?"

"No, they're sort of scattered now, but mostly back east."

"Big family?"

"Three brothers and two sisters, more nieces and nephews than I can keep track of."

"But no kids of your own?"

"No, not yet."

"Do you want children?" It should have been a first-date question. She shouldn't waste her time with a man who would never accept Aiden.

"Oh, yes," he said emphatically, "with the right woman," and he gave her an intimidatingly sexy grin. "I'd like to have the kind of family my parents did—big and noisy. Are you an only child?"

"I have a brother, Richard. He sells insurance and coaches Little League in Los Angeles."

"He sounds nice and boring."

"A little boring, but he's a good guy."

"Sometimes boring is good." It was something Teresa's mother said, and it made her feel even more relaxed.

The movie was definitely not boring. During a particularly tense scene, Frank's hand closed on hers, and she felt something like gratitude. After the first date kiss, she had had visions of movie dates from high school that had developed into total grab fests, but this was nothing like that. His hand was warm and comforting. They were two adults watching a very gripping movie and enjoying it together.

When it was over, they headed for the lobby in

complete silence, and then he said, "Wow!"

"Yeah," she said. "It was great." She was slightly tearful and afraid he would think she was silly, but he squeezed her hand in sympathy.

"So what do you think?" he asked. "Pizza?"

"Pizza would be perfect."

"More perfect than the Perfect Place, anyway?"

She laughed. "It was nice too, but pizza goes better with a movie."

Discussing what they'd seen and munching pizza at the nearby Tony's was so much fun they stayed longer than they had intended, and Teresa was afraid Chelsea would be angry or worried. "I'm sure she'll be glad of the overtime," Frank said. "I'll pay her a little extra."

"No—that's my job!" she protested.

"Nonsense, it's much easier for me, and you know it. I'll drive her home too."

"She has her bicycle."

"A bicycle? This time of night?"

"She has a light, and she lives just down the road. I can watch her most of the way from my front porch."

"Still, a young girl alone after dark?"

"This is Cougar, not the big city. It's safe."

"Oh, yeah? Tell it to the families of Wade Linedecker's victims."

"They weren't killed here," she objected.

"Two of them weren't. The third we don't know about—she hasn't been identified, and Linedecker claims he didn't kill her. He's probably just trying to keep from further incriminating himself, but..."

"Well, that's a little unsettling, but I'm sure Chelsea will be fine."

Somehow the discussion about safety distracted her

from the payment issue, and while she reminded Chelsea to be careful, Frank folded bills into the girl's hand. "I'll be glad to drive you home if you like," he said.

"No, thanks," she said blithely, gathered her books, and headed out the door. "'Bye, Mrs. Lansing."

They stood on the porch until she was out of sight, and then he took Teresa's hand and gave her a quick, pepperoni-spicy kiss. "Can I stay?" he asked.

"No, Frank. It was a wonderful evening. Thank you for everything."

"Come on," he coaxed. He kissed her again, this time with an intensity that left her both shaken and wanting more. His hand was on her breast, and he was pressed up against her. "You want to," he said. "You know you do."

She did, or part of her did. "No, I don't," she said, laughing, trying to keep things light.

"Yeah, you do." He caressed her cheek and kissed her again. "You make me crazy. It's been such a great evening. Let's not end it here."

"I'm afraid we have to."

He kissed her again. "Come on, Teresa." He said her name in a caressing way, as if it was the tenderest of endearments.

"No, Frank. It's too soon. Keep in mind I have a little boy in the house who is still sad about a previous breakup."

"He can't hear us," he reminded her.

"No, but he might get up in the night with a bad dream or something."

"Does he do that a lot?"

"No," she admitted, "almost never, but—"

"We could lock the door," he said. He didn't sound entirely serious, as if he were teasing, but she didn't think he was. "If he comes knocking, I'll hide in the closet."

"My closet is very crowded," she said, trying to match his tone.

"So it's a no? You're shutting me down?"

"Yes, Frank."

He let her go. "You did with the schoolteacher, though, right?"

"I can't think of any reason why I would want to answer that question," she said. She was afraid she sounded self-righteous or angry. She wasn't, but she needed him to know where she drew the lines.

"Yeah, okay," he said. "I can see I need to earn this. I'd better take my bad self home. Good night, Teresa."

"Good night, Frank."

When he was gone, she went in to check on Aiden. He was sleeping peacefully, one hand tucked under his cheek, his soft blond hair rumpled. She bent to kiss the top of his head. "You're the man in my life," she whispered. "I don't need anybody else."

Still, it did feel good to be wanted again, after feeling so bruised by Brett's infidelity.

Chapter 5

The mail was delivered before Teresa left for work on Monday, including a small package addressed in familiar handwriting. She opened it, exasperated but curious. It was a CD, the Johnny Nash version of "Tears on My Pillow."

"Brett, you big dope!" she said out loud. She played it while she folded the towels, still warm from the dryer. The lyrics didn't fit their situation—she hadn't walked out of his life to his best friend. She had chosen her son over his worthless hide, though, and Brett and Aiden had been very good friends. And the rest…well, he should have thought of that sooner. She hoped he wasn't going to be a nuisance. As always, her first impulse was to tell Alix, her confidant in everything. She called her immediately, while the mournful song was still playing in the background.

"Can you believe it?" she asked.

"Crocodile tears," Alix pronounced. "Never mind dopey Brett. How was your da-a-ate?"

"It was good. A lot of fun."

"Yeah, but how *was* it?"

"It was good."

"You didn't do it—did you?"

"No, but he wanted to. He said he was an adrenaline junkie; maybe he likes the thrill of the chase. I'll tell you what, between him and Brett, I haven't been this popular since I had a new bike in the third grade!"

"A red one with streamers on the handles."

"And you were so jealous." It was the great thing about talking to Alix. She got every reference, shared every memory.

"Was not. So, whaddya think?"

Teresa sighed. "I don't know. I don't know what to make of him. We have the same taste in movies, which is nice, and he's easy to talk to. He can be funny and sweet too—plus he's very sexy."

"Yeah, he is kind of easy on the eyes."

"Are you jealous?"

"No, no, I'm through with all of that."

"I thought I was too."

"Yeah, be careful. You know what they say about the rebound."

"He acts like he really likes me, but I keep thinking this is the guy in the Mary Higgins Clark novel who turns out to be the serial killer."

"Yeah, or your long-lost brother."

"Eww! I'll keep that in mind next time. He's a cop, so he's probably not a serial killer, right? He would have had to pass a background check?"

"Which only means he didn't get caught. No telling what he got away with. Don't let him cut your head off—it's so messy."

Alix could always make her laugh.

****

Frank called Tuesday evening when she had just gotten home from work, still damp from a sudden shower of rain. Thunder rumbled in the distance while she struggled to sound intelligent and composed instead of flustered and tongue-tied. "Are you busy?" he asked.

"I'm about to be," she said. Aiden was putting groceries away in all the wrong places. Was there ever a time when a single mother *wasn't* busy?

"I'll be quick, then. Have you ever been to Grey Harbor?"

"My dad used to have a fishing boat, and he took me out from there once."

"You know how to fish?" He was impressed.

"Not really, but I did catch something that day. I forget what it was, but it was big, and a seal took a bite out of it before I could reel it in." Sun suddenly slanted through the kitchen window, and she held the phone against her shoulder and signed to Aiden, "Look for rainbow." She pointed toward the east-facing front door, and he ran into the living room.

"How old were you?" Frank asked.

"I don't remember."

"Well, I think it's time you went back—to Grey Harbor, I mean, not fishing. I thought we could take your boy up and spend the weekend. It would be a good chance for me to get to know him, and we could have a great time. Kids like the beach, right? We could even visit the cove where the seals are."

Teresa couldn't think what she should object to first. "The weekend?" she said. "I think it's still too soon—for Aiden, I mean. A brief meeting would be better first, and—"

"It would be a lot of fun for him, though, Teresa, and I'm not going to push anything, I promise. It would be very low-key, just hanging out. They have a very nice hotel with three-queen loft rooms—two queen beds downstairs and one up in a loft. I thought he would think it was fun—being up there—and the view is great, and the hotel has little windows we can leave open all night so we can hear the surf."

"Mama!" Aiden called.

"It sounds nice, but I don't think we should take him anywhere together yet."

He was silent for a second before he said, "You know best, I'm sure. How about if the two of us go this weekend, and if you like it we can do it another time with the boy."

"Overnight?"

"Yes, there's a lot to see, and it's a long drive home after dark. It would be much more relaxing to take our time."

"Mama! Rainbow!"

"I don't think—"

"Come on, it will be fun. No pressure, I promise. Two beds. Nothing will happen unless you want it to. We can even get a loft room, and you can sleep upstairs."

"Mama!" Aiden called loudly enough that Frank must have heard.

She felt pulled in two directions and couldn't think clearly or she might not have said, "Yes, all right. I have to go, Frank."

The rainbow was spectacular.

****

As soon as Aiden was in bed, she called Alix. "We-ell," Alix said skeptically. "I think you should go if you want to, but don't kid yourself nothing is going to happen."

"His original plan was to have Aiden with us, though."

"Maybe you should take him. He could be your

little chaperone."

"That's not his job, and I don't want him to be stuck spending a whole weekend with a man he doesn't know. Frank is kind of a strong personality, and he doesn't know anything about kids. It could be a disaster."

"Do *you* want to spend a whole weekend with a man you barely know, a man with a strong personality and a shitload of testosterone?"

"I don't have a clue! I feel like I need to slow this down, but at the same time…I always wondered what this would be like—a whirlwind romance, being swept off my feet. It's exciting, but is it real? I sort of want to find out. It's probably bullshit, but being courted is nice. What I don't want is to be away from my son so long. Weekends are very important."

"He'll survive. Mama has to have some fun too. You can be a better mom if you take care of yourself first. I'll think of something cool for him and Sasha to do, and he won't even miss you."

"But you'll be at the grill in the evening, and—"

"We'll work it out—if you want to go. If you don't, just explain about Aiden. If he's going to romance single mothers, he should learn to be patient where the kids are concerned."

"I'm not sure I should have gone out with him the first time. It's too soon after Brett. I don't know what to do. I like him, but he's trying to go too fast for me."

"So speak up for yourself. Repeat after me: Frank, you're moving too fast for me."

"I said I would go."

"So unsay it. If it pisses him off, he'll leave you alone. If it was meant to be, he'll come back when you're ready."

Teresa sighed. "You always make it sound so simple."

"Because it is. Oh, I love running your love life. It's so much less messy than having my own."

"I've never spent even one night with any man except Gene and Brett—and you know they didn't move this fast."

"Well, kiddo, if you don't want to go too far, just don't shave your legs."

Teresa laughed. She felt better, but she knew nothing was settled.

****

She called Frank the next day. He was at work but said he wasn't busy and it was a good time to talk. She wanted to negotiate. He had in mind spending the whole weekend at the coast, going late Friday and coming back early Sunday evening. It would be too much for Aiden, and it was too long for her to be away from him—longer than she ever had been. She suggested they drive over Saturday morning, not too early, and come back Sunday afternoon. He sounded relaxed and quickly put her at ease, and once again she found him almost too easy to talk to. She ended up telling him almost the entire conversation with Alix.

He laughed. "Nothing you do is going to piss me off," he said warmly. "I told you I'm the tenacious kind. And I don't want to rush you—we'll take it at your pace, always. It's totally up to you. I had a head start—before you even noticed I was around. And just so you know: you don't have to shave anything for me."

"I can't believe I told you that! It's a girl secret."

"Believe it or not, I've heard it before. I have two sisters, remember? And I was married. Question is: do you want *me* to shave? I hear some women like it scratchy."

Teresa laughed. "This is a very bizarre conversation."

"Yeah, it is—and I gotta go." He hung up. He *was* at work, after all.

She had second thoughts—lots of them. She worried and wondered. What she didn't do was pick up the phone and cancel. Frank must have made a reservation by now—a hotel like the one he had described was bound to be booked up early. She saw no way to back out—unless Aiden got sick—and she needed to trust Frank's promise to follow her lead. She needed to relax and let herself have fun.

****

On Thursday, she was doing inventory at the vet clinic when she heard a tentative rap on the door. Veronica wouldn't have knocked, and clients shouldn't have been back there, but she didn't want to stop what she was doing and said, "Come in," without looking up.

The door opened halfway, and a familiar voice said, "It's me—hat in hand." Brett. He opened it the rest of the way and added, "Except I don't wear a hat."

"I'm working, Brett."

"I know. I'm sorry, but you won't let me see Aiden, and this is the only other place—I really need to talk to you."

"We have nothing to say. And don't send me stuff—it's just embarrassing to both of us."

He shook his head. "When did you get so hard?"

"When you screwed Lacey Norman."

He winced. "I was drunk. I—"

That made her mad. "How many times did we agree you are responsible, legally and morally, for whatever you do after you choose to consume alcohol?"

"I know, I know. It was wrong. It was bad. It was stupid. I hate that I did it. I hate knowing I hurt you."

"And Aiden."

"Yes, and Aiden. You have a perfect right to be angry. But I love you, Reesie."

"Stop it."

"I can't. I'm fighting for my life."

"For something that's already over."

"I don't believe that." The rain was suddenly loud against the window, and Teresa turned her head, distracted. She could think only that if the bad weather kept up, the weekend with Frank might be spoiled. Had she distanced herself from Brett that much? She had been overwhelmed with anger at first, but now maybe she was over it. Maybe Brett was right; she had become hard, callused.

"What?" She couldn't remember what he had been saying.

He looked confused and then tried again to say what he had come to say. "I've been in exile because of what I did, and I know I deserved it, but I didn't think it would be forever. I'll do whatever you want, but—"

"I want," she said emphatically, evenly, "for you to leave now. I'm working. Stop bothering me."

He didn't move. "I miss you both so much," he said. "I love you."

She didn't want to hear it. She didn't want to believe it. "Get out," she said. Unexpected tears blinded her, and when she could see again, Brett was gone.

Chapter 6

It rained Friday night, but Saturday morning the valley was clear and sunny. Teresa turned on the news to check the weather report for the coast. It wasn't very informative—partly cloudy, temperature in the mid sixties. Clouds were all too common—they had given Grey Harbor its name—but at least it shouldn't be too cold. She put a light sweater and a warm sweatshirt in her overnight bag.

She had put an annoying amount of thought into her packing. Which pairs of jeans were in best condition? Which T-shirts were most flattering? Should she take a blouse in case they ate at the hotel or an expensive restaurant? A lacy nightgown to look fetching in or pajamas for modesty? What she needed was to be firmly in control of the situation, not to dither like a teenage girl before the junior prom.

Frank was right on time, as always. He grinned at her, happy and relaxed, and took her bag. He pretended to find it heavy and put it in the back seat. "I hope you have a bathing suit in there," he said.

She shook her head. "I did pack shorts and a halter top for the beach, but it might be too cold. It's been a while since I wore my bathing suit. It probably wouldn't fit me."

He shook his head. "I bet you haven't gained a pound since high school."

"You'd lose the bet. I had a baby, Frank."

"Yeah, I guess you did, but it doesn't show." He opened the passenger door for her. He had a bag, smaller than hers, and an open-top cardboard box in the back seat. She could see sunscreen, an insulated cooler bag, and the red cross of a first-aid kit in the box. He had thought of everything.

He got in, glanced at her to be sure she had her seatbelt on, and started the car. "Tell me about him," he said. "Your boy."

"Aiden," she said. "I don't think you've ever used his name."

"I guess—it's one of those cute, modern names. Sort of trendy?"

"It's also a very old Irish name."

"Did you choose it?"

"I think it was pretty mutual. We considered a lot of names and decided we liked it best."

"So what's he like—Aiden?"

"Shy with new people," she said, "but pretty fearless in other ways. Smart. He's already a good reader, and he picked up sign language really fast. "

"Was he born deaf?"

"No, they think it was from a high fever."

"So it's not genetic. That's good. I looked up some stuff on cochlear implants. I guess it's a better option when they're not born deaf, but the sooner the better, right?"

"They say nine is the upper limit for the best outcome, but even adults can benefit."

"We'll have to see what we can do," he said, as if it were nothing. "I know some doctors—we might be able to work something out."

"We? You haven't even met him!" He was only trying to be nice, but he had skipped several steps in their relationship without her permission.

"We'll talk about it another time," he said soothingly. "Does he see his dad?"

"No," she said shortly. "It's better that way."

"You would know," he said and then changed the subject. "I thought we'd head straight to Genoa and work our way up the coast. Stop wherever we want— I'd like to see the lighthouses and the aquarium and so on. We could go whale watching or, you know, whatever you'd like. I aim to please."

Teresa gestured toward the cooler bag in the back seat. "Did you pack a lunch?"

"No, just bottled water and snack bars, in case, but there are lots of good places to eat. They cater to tourists, so jeans are fine. You look very pretty today, by the way. That's a good color for you. Cute shoes, too."

Teresa laughed. "Who told you to say that?"

"What do you mean?" he asked, but his feigned innocence was clearly a joke.

"Somebody told you women like it if you compliment their shoes. These are for comfort, not fashion."

"I told you I knew a lot of girl secrets. But let's make a pact—no bullshit between us."

"That works for me."

"Okay, I didn't really notice your shoes, but it is a good color on you, and you look prettier every time I see you. I'm secretly hoping it's because of me. I'm easily deluded."

"Sounds like bullshit to me," she said, laughing. "I

wear T-shirts most of the time because they're cheap and comfortable, but I also like them. They have a lot of scope for self-expression. They can show where you've been or what you think. This one—"

"Is blue, which I know is your favorite color."

"Yes, and I like butterflies, but it also has a religious message."

"Beauty abounds?"

"Oh, you *are* observant. That, in a nutshell, is my entire religious philosophy. The universe is so full of beauty that you can only stand in awe. I try to look for it every day, wherever I am." She was a little embarrassed to have been so candid about something so personal, but he had asked for no bullshit.

"I think we're headed in the right direction, then," he said. "Did you see the rainbow the other day? It was right after I talked to you."

"Yes, it was beautiful."

"I thought maybe it was an omen. Does that sound dumb?"

"A SWAT cop who believes in omens? Not at all."

"Oh, trust me, cops are very superstitious. I'll take you to a police bar sometime and introduce you to some of my friends—rabbit's feet, lucky charms, you name it."

"I don't blame them. It's dangerous, what you do."

"Everything is dangerous if you're careless. Training, preparation, focus, attention to detail—you do the job right, and it's a walk in the park."

"Which I wouldn't do after dark."

"Yes, and you could get bitten by a rabid dog."

"I have had a few cat scratches, but nobody shoots at me."

"Nobody is shooting at anybody today. My phone isn't even on—somebody's covering for me this weekend—and all we have to do is relax and look for the beauty." He gestured toward the trees lining the road. "You ain't seen nothin' yet," he said.

Teresa was feeling more relaxed by the minute. "Beauty isn't only visual," she said. "How 'bout some music?"

Frank touched something on the steering wheel. "What would you like? I have about seventy music stations on this thing. Pop, rock, country, gospel, jazz, classical—pick a decade."

"This is a lot of car," she said admiringly. "Do you mind country?"

"I like country—how about this?" He touched the center screen on the dashboard, and the interior was flooded with rich sound. She recognized the voice of Kris Kristofferson. "Outlaw country for a girl nicknamed Terror."

"I think we just might be compatible," she said.

****

The weather was overcast and cool at the coast. Genoa was the home of the Oceanfront Aquarium, which Teresa had visited once as a child, but it had been enlarged since then and was far more impressive. Strolling through it, hand in hand with Frank, she said, "Aiden would love this!"

"Next time," he said comfortably.

She had no trouble finding beauty here—floor-to-ceiling tanks of clear blue water filled with darting, shining fish of every color and pattern, intricate coral formations, and her favorite sea anemones. "Look at this one!" she exclaimed, pointing out a very bright yellow fish. She almost turned around to find Aiden and call his attention to it. Had it been too long since she had done anything like this without him? Studying the hermit crabs, she said, "He would even like these ugly things."

"You miss him." It was matter-of-fact, neither censure nor sympathy.

"Yes," she admitted, "I'm a mom pretty much 24/7. It's hard to turn off."

"Don't try," he said. "We'll get something for him in the gift shop."

"Thanks for understanding," she said, "and I did appreciate you wanting to include him."

She didn't see anything suitable in the gift shop and was browsing through the postcards when Frank came over with a T-shirt—"Look at this; they change colors in the sunlight. What size would he wear?"

"Six or eight." She automatically checked the price tag.

"I've got it," he said. He showed her another shirt. "Which would he like—sharks or seahorses?"

"Sharks, but Frank—"

"I've got it," he said again and turned away. When she came up to him at the cash register, he already had his credit card out, and he took the postcards she had selected out of her hand and added them to his purchases—not one, but two child-size T-shirts, a stuffed clown fish, and a light blue V-neck with a sea anemone design.

She didn't want to make a scene in the store, but outside she said, "You can't keep doing this."

"Okay," he said, "let's have this discussion and get it out of the way. I have money. I like to spend it. I like spending it on people I care about. You are struggling to make ends meet on a nothing salary, far less than you deserve. It makes me happy to buy things for you. I know you don't want to feel obligated, but you don't have to. This is a no-cost, no-obligation trip. The money I'm spending is nothing to me—it's like I offered you a glass of water. Time is valuable. Money is not."

"It is when you don't have it."

"But I do. I can throw it away and not even think about it. Spending money to make people happy is the only way to give it value. Spending time with me, precious time you could spend with your son, is a great gift. *I* owe *you*. And please believe this—I know the difference between a woman like you and someone who can be bought. You are not obliged to do anything except relax and have a good time."

She took a deep breath. She wanted to protest, but what could she say? He seemed so sincere, so plausible. She did feel obligated, but she wouldn't do anything she didn't want to because of it. "Okay," she said finally. "I'll try. How did you know I liked the sea anemones?"

"Oh, I have my ways!" He took her hand. "Shall we head down to the beach? I think it's a little bit rocky here, but the view is worth it."

"Okay," she said again. They went back to the car, and Teresa took her camera out of her bag. Frank gave it a critical glance. "I know it's not fancy," she said, trying not to sound apologetic, "but I like simple. Point and shoot."

"I use my phone," he said. "Let me see yours."

"My phone?" He nodded, and she dug it out of her

purse.

He raised an eyebrow. "Pretty basic," he said. "Can you even text on that thing?"

"No, but—"

"I'll buy you a new one," he said. "We'll get one for Aiden, too. If he's learning to read, he can learn to text. It would be a great way for you to communicate with him."

"Frank!" She stood rooted to the ground. "Back up! You're going too far!"

She was afraid he would be angry, thinking this was the point he had already made, but he grinned. "You are a terror," he said. "It's okay—keep drawing your lines. I like you better for it." He kissed her quickly, lightly, and took her hand again.

After admiring the panorama from the beach, they hiked back up. As they got into the car, he glanced at his watch. "We should decide where to eat lunch," he said. "There's a good seafood place here, or we could go a little farther. He nodded toward the glove compartment. "You'll find a map in there. Look and see which is closer—Oxhead Lighthouse or Seal Cove."

Teresa obediently opened the glove compartment. "I would have thought a fancy car like this would have GPS."

"It does. It's programmed for Grey Harbor. The map should be right in front."

It was. So was a pair of handcuffs. She held them up and handed the map to him. "You don't have a gun in here, do you?" she asked.

"No, but there's riot gear in the trunk."

"Really?" It made his job seem very real. She was still dangling the handcuffs. "I've always been kind of fascinated by these," she said.

He looked up from the map. "You mean like *Fifty Shades of Grey*?"

She laughed. "No. I haven't read it, but no, nothing like that. Maybe it's the romance of police work."

"It's not very romantic in real life," he said, "but I could try those on you sometime."

"No, thanks." She hoped he was joking.

"Let's go on up to the lighthouse," he said, refolding the map. "The restaurant close by is a good one, if I remember rightly."

"Good like the Perfect Place?"

"No, no lobster linguini. More like sandwiches and tacos."

They drove north, stopping twice to take pictures of ocean views. It was noon when they pulled up in front of the Ox Head Family Restaurant. The name of the lighthouse was derived from the shape of the headland it sat on, but the restaurant décor was more literal, with steer horns everywhere. It was very casual, with bench seating, wooden tables, and plenty of families in evidence.

Teresa looked automatically at the children's menu, which included peanut-butter-and-jelly sandwiches as well as macaroni and cheese, and then decided on the tuna melt. It came with French fries, which she almost never allowed herself. Frank chose fish and chips. It all proved delicious, and they found another trait in common—generous use of catsup on the thick, salty French fries and stopping as soon as they were no longer hot.

Afterward in the gift shop, Frank wanted to buy Aiden a toy shark. "It would be too much of a good thing," she told him firmly. "He's not used to so much all at once."

"Maybe it's time you both got used to it," he said, but he put the shark back on the shelf. He continued to browse while she visited the ladies' room, and when they got to the car he slipped a bracelet onto her wrist. It wasn't anything expensive, just blue glass beads strung on elastic.

"I couldn't help it," he said. "It reminded me of you. But then, everything reminds me of you."

"Don't say things like that," she protested lightly. "Thank you. It's very pretty. Next time I get to buy you something."

"Oh, I can't wait to see what you'll pick out," he said. "It could be very revealing."

They climbed the long, winding flight of stairs to the lighthouse. The view from the top was breathtaking. The sun was breaking through the cloud cover, and the water sparkled with glittering light. "How's this for beauty?" he asked.

They toured the keeper's house and climbed the narrow steps to the light. Slightly breathless from the ascent, they leaned on the parapet and surveyed the ocean view. A strong breeze ruffled their hair. "It's so peaceful way up above everything like this," Teresa said. Just then a group of youngsters crowded through the door from the stairwell, talking loudly, tinny sounds leaking from their earbuds.

Frank and Teresa laughed and headed back down, hands linked companionably. They stopped in the gift shop but bought only postcards. The sun was definitely warmer outside when they emerged. "I think it's going to be nice after all," he said. "Maybe we should try to get to Grey Harbor early and spend some time on the beach. We could even go sailing."

"Whatever you want," she said. She felt, if not reckless, at least ready for what the day might bring.

They stopped at Seal Cove but didn't stay long. It had a balcony for whale watching, but no sightings had been made for two days, and the seals were drowsing in the sun. In the gift shop, Teresa bought Frank a coffee mug with a spouting whale design because she liked the color. He seemed pleased with her choice.

Chapter 7

When they arrived in Grey Harbor, it was sunny and warmer. Frank gestured toward a small shopping center and suggested they could buy Teresa a new bathing suit, but she declined. "Shall we see if we can check in early and use the room to change for the beach?" he suggested.

Teresa hesitated. It was early enough to cancel the reservation, enjoy more of the sights, and drive back to Cougar tonight. It would still have been a good time, and she would be with Aiden tonight and not at risk for making a fool of herself. Was that what she was afraid of? He had insisted there would be no pressure, but he had tried to talk his way into her bedroom after their second date—did she really believe they could spend a night in the same room without anything happening? If she said yes now, would she be consenting to everything else that could follow, as Brett had when he drank the first beer that led to his infidelity?

But of course she would not be cheating on Brett—the relationship was over; he was the past. Frank was very possibly the future. I'm an adult, she reminded herself. I'm in control. "Okay," she said.

He had noticed her hesitation. "Are you sure? If you'd rather do something else—"

"No, it's fine." If they couldn't check in until later, she would take it as a sign—he wasn't the only one who believed in omens.

They were able to check in right away. The hotel stretched along the shoreline, three floors high and only one room wide, so every room had an ocean view. Their room was on the second floor, and it was large and comfortable, with two queen beds, a fireplace with a TV mounted above it, a mini-fridge and microwave, and a plush couch and chairs. The western wall was largely glass, with sliding doors leading to a balcony overlooking the beach. Frank slid back the small window above them to let in the soothing sound of the surf.

"Which bed do you want?" he asked. Teresa indicated the one nearest the door.

"Are you sure? This one is closer to the view."

"This one is closer to the bathroom," she said. She put her bag on the bed and checked out the bathroom. It was very nice, with a deep tub and deluxe shower head. The whole arrangement was cozier than she had expected, with a slightly rustic charm, and it made her feel a little more relaxed. She went back for her bag and said, "I'll change in the bathroom."

She put on her denim shorts and halter top, slathered on sunscreen, and studied herself critically in the mirror. Her shoulders and legs were too pale, and she had put on a few pounds since high school. She had never minded before; she wouldn't want to be some anorexic stick. Brett had liked her the way she was—at least until he succumbed to Lacey Norman's more voluptuous charms.

When she came out of the bathroom, Frank was wearing swimming trunks and putting on sunscreen. He looked at her and smiled. "Oh, I like that," he said. "I think it's more becoming than a bikini." He held out the tube. "Do my back, and I'll do yours?"

She spread the fragrant cream on his back and shoulders, feeling the firm, well-defined muscles beneath. He was altogether too attractive with this much bare skin showing. When she was done, she turned around and let him return the favor. He accomplished the task quickly and almost impersonally, but it made her feel little shivers of pleasure.

As they went out, she couldn't resist taking a last look at herself in the full-length mirror near the door, and he said, "Mirror, mirror on the wall, who's the fairest of them all?"

The beach access was only steps away from the hotel, down an easy flight of stairs. The sand was thick and warm and then, farther out, packed hard and pleasantly damp under their bare feet. They walked down to the water's edge to test the temperature—it was cold enough to be invigorating. At first they only waded along the edge, the small waves breaking around their ankles, but soon enough they were splashing each other and laughing. Teresa meant to just get her feet wet, but in no time at all she was soaked and conscious of her shorts and top clinging to her skin. They gradually ventured farther out. Teresa was a strong swimmer, and she wasn't afraid, but it occurred to her this was a metaphor—she was getting in deeper and deeper.

When they were tired of the water, they sat on the rocks and let the sun dry their clothes. The beach was not crowded, but there were plenty of people around. Families, couples, lone joggers, and groups of young people passed where they sat. He pointed out an unusual group of rock formations about half a mile away and suggested they walk up the beach to look at them.

They ambled slowly, hand in hand, talking about inconsequentials. A young Asian couple stopped them and asked if they would take their picture with the ocean in the background. Frank took the camera, snapped the picture, and engaged them in conversation about the camera's features. "Would you recommend it?" he asked. "My lady might be in the market for a new one."

My lady. She was still having a little trouble processing the offhand reference when he took her hand and they moved on. They stopped again when a group of boys throwing a football around let it get away from them. Frank scooped it up and kicked it back to them with impressive control. "Is there anything you aren't good at?" she asked.

He looked at her, surprised, and then smiled. "Yes, but I'm trying not to let you find out about them."

"Why?" she asked. "I wouldn't want you to be perfect."

The rock formations were indeed interesting, bigger at the top than at the base, where the waves had eroded them. They encountered a lot of driftwood and seaweed and no other people, so the spot had a very appealing wild beauty.

By the time they made their way back, the marine layer was beginning to drift in, and the beach was nearly deserted. They walked more slowly than before, and Frank draped his arm around Teresa's shoulders and pulled her close. "Everything okay?" he asked.

"Lovely," she said. "Thank you."

"What would you like to do for dinner? The hotel restaurant is good—not too fancy—or we could try somewhere else, or call room service."

"Whatever you want," she said again.

"Let's do room service," he decided. "And go out for breakfast. Or would you prefer breakfast in bed?"

"No," she said, "room service sounds fine. Breakfast is my favorite meal to eat out."

He was more pleased than surprised. "Me too."

"We may be passing the great compatibility test," she joked.

When they got back to the room, Teresa called Alix to check on Aiden. Alix gave him the phone so he could say, "Night, Mama." He sounded cheerful enough, but his voice brought tears to her eyes.

Alix came back on. "He says to tell you—wait, wait—I can't keep up. Oh, okay—never mind, he can tell you everything when you get back. Everything is fine. He's happy as a clam. How's it going?"

"Fine," she said firmly. "I'll call you tomorrow." When she hung up, Frank was watching her. He put a comforting hand on the back of her neck and kissed her forehead. "She says he's fine," she said, "but I'm not sure. You were right; it would be great if we could text."

"Next time we'll have him with us," he said. "Good thing, too. I understand he has to get used to the idea of me, but I don't think it's healthy for you to leave him with the bartender so much."

"Alix isn't a bartender," Teresa objected. "She owns the grill, and she's my best friend."

"Maybe so, but I noticed she uses some pretty rough language at times. I don't think she's the best influence. And her little girl has no manners. She could be bullying the boy."

Teresa bristled. "So says the great childrearing expert."

He chose to be amused. "Got your dander up," he said. "I just think it will be better to include him next time. I'm sure he could use a good male role model, too."

"He had Brett..."

"And look how that turned out."

"So, okay, what's *your* parenting philosophy?"

"My pare—? I'm sure you'd know best."

"You're not one of those guys who expect little boys to man up all the time?"

"No, I'm not that guy either. Even if your ex is right and you're a little overprotective, I would never interfere."

"I'm not overprotective." She tried to sound calm and sure, not defensive.

"I didn't say you were," he said soothingly. "Shall we look at the room service menu?"

They'd both had fish and fries for lunch, so they ordered Beachfront burgers with chili and coleslaw. While they waited for the food, they sat on the balcony and watched the sunset. It was pretty spectacular, the pink-and-blue sky mirrored on the water, the white foam of the waves glowing against the darkening ocean. Their chairs were about a foot apart, and Frank took Teresa's hand. "I want to meet your son," he said. "What do you think he would like to do?"

She considered. "He did want to go to Oktoberfest..."

"Isn't it all beer and—"

"No, it's more like a local fair. The beer garden is separate, and you have to be twenty-one to get in. They have live music and booths and rides for the kids. Brett was planning to take us."

"It sounds perfect," he said. "Casual, low key—we could meet as if by chance. If he isn't comfortable around me, we can go our separate ways without making a big deal of it."

"Thank you," she said. He moved his chair closer and put his arm around her.

The food was wonderful, the burgers big and juicy, the chili piping hot. The sun and salt air had made them hungry, and they relished every bite. They ate slowly, talking comfortably as they watched the last remnants of sunlight fade. When they were finished, Frank put his hand on the back of Teresa's neck and kneaded gently. "You're still thinking about Aiden," he said. "You're a little tense."

"No, I'm not," she said, but not very convincingly.

"Tell you what," he said. "Lie on your stomach on the bed, and I'll give you the super-special, world-famous McAllister massage."

She laughed, but she got up and lay on her bed. He switched off the lamp between the beds, softening the light in the room. He sat on the edge of the bed and started slowly, rubbing her neck and running his fingers through her hair. After a minute he moved so he was straddling her and dug the fingers of both hands into her scalp, her neck, and her shoulders. It was wonderful, sending shivers of pleasure through her. She had had massage therapy once after a pulled muscle, and this was very much the same, at least at first. The therapist had played soft music in the background, but here the constant, soothing sound of the ocean relaxed her more than any music would.

His hands moved down her bare back. They were warm and comforting. Her scalp tingled, and her muscles relaxed under his fingers. She lay with her cheek on her folded arms and let herself drift a little. His hands slid under the waistband of her shorts and massaged deeply. Teresa sighed with pleasure. He moved farther down, stroking her legs. "This is great," she said gratefully. "I should do you now."

"Don't worry about me," he said softly. "This is only about you. I want you to relax. I want you to trust me." He continued, taking first one foot and then the other in both hands for an all-over massage. It was the best part yet, and she murmured with pleasure.

"Turn over," he said. She did. He smiled into her eyes, and after a moment she had to look away. "Relax," he said. She closed her eyes, and he took her face in his hands and caressed it, gently at first and then more firmly, continuing the massage. The therapist had never done this side of her. It was delicious. His hands moved on to her throat and her bare shoulders. His fingers slid under the halter strap and down to the neckline. Because of the bare back she wasn't wearing a bra. This was another line she should draw— therapists didn't cross it—but she didn't say anything.

From the beginning this had been more sensuous than sexual, but now it was getting more personal by the minute. His hands were on her breasts, at first through the fabric and then underneath, stroking and cradling. She was neither frightened nor aroused, but he was very definitely making her feel something strong and deep. She held her breath, and he said, "Relax," again. He finally moved on, his hands warm on her bare midriff and her belly, down inside her shorts. Teresa moaned softly.

Draw a line, she told herself, but she didn't stop him. She was being manipulated, but she liked what he was doing. He moved on to her upper thighs, deeply kneading muscles that were a little tired from the beach, and on down her legs, with briefer attention to her feet this time, and back up the insides of her calves and thighs. One hand slipped between her legs. It was both an unpressured, natural continuation of the ritual and very deeply arousing.

She opened her eyes and looked into his. "This is supposed to relax me?" she asked.

"Yes." His hands were still now.

"This is supposed to make me trust you?" The thing was, she really wanted to trust him.

"Yes. Are you relaxed? Are you ready to go to sleep? Do you want me to kiss you good night and get in the other bed?"

She wanted to say yes, and she thought he would accept it, but she didn't. When she didn't answer, he took her face in his hands again and kissed her, not for goodnight, but deeply, intensely, and for a long time. Damn, he was good! "I love you," he said.

"It's too soon," she protested, but in the moment, still tingling from the massage, with the sound of the surf under everything, she felt something very like love. She had never been so ready for anything in her life. I can't be bought, she thought, but it seems I can be seduced.

****

Teresa turned her head toward the sound of the

surf. They hadn't closed the drapes, and she could see the moonlight, diffused by the overcast, touching the waves. She could hear Frank breathing, and when she stirred, he put his hand on her neck and kissed her shoulder. "You are something else," he said. She turned to look at him, and he smiled. He was lying on his side, propped on one elbow, looking down at her admiringly. "You were with me all the way, weren't you?" She didn't know what to say and just nodded. He touched her lightly, stroked her shoulder, and kissed her gently on the lips and then on the forehead. "Was it like that with Devlin?" he asked.

Teresa sat up abruptly. "We are not having a discussion about him," she said. It was one line she could definitely draw. She was still wearing her halter top, a little askew, but she had lost track of her shorts. Unbidden, a memory surfaced—the first time with Brett, he had thanked her, as if she had done him a favor. He had been so sweet to her, but that was in the past. "I don't want to hear about other women you've been with either," she said.

Frank sat up too and put his arm around her. "There haven't been too many," he said. "I'm more of a one-woman man. I'm sorry if the question bothered you; I was just curious."

"Or you wanted me to stroke your ego."

He was amused. "Teresa the Terror," he said.

"What was your wife like?" she asked. She could be curious too. "I *don't* mean in bed," she added. When he hesitated, she said, "I'm sorry—do you mind talking about her? Is it too painful?"

He shrugged. "She was like you in some ways, but tougher. You have a softness and vulnerability I find very attractive. She was gutsy, energetic…"

"How did she die?"

"An accident," he said grimly.

Teresa rubbed his arm sympathetically. "I'm sorry," she said.

"It's in the past," he said firmly. He looked at her. "Did Devlin treat you all right? I mean besides…"

"Yes, and I guess he didn't want out of the relationship. He's trying to get me to take him back, but I told him to cut his losses."

"Did you tell him about us?"

She shook her head.

"It might be kinder; cut the cord once and for all."

"I wasn't sure we had anything to tell yet," she said. She pulled away a little. "Hey, I thought we weren't going to talk about exes."

"You're right. This should be all about you." He kissed her cheek. "What would you like to do now? We could go down to the beach again or go out for dessert or stay here and…talk." He grinned.

Teresa was half distracted now, trying to figure out how she felt about all of this. She didn't answer, and he put his arms around her and held her close. She was relaxed and comfortable now, but wasn't this all happening too fast? She was having second thoughts she should have had first. "I'd like to take a shower," she said. She could feel the grit of sand under her top, and hot water always made her feel refreshed.

"Alone?"

"Alone."

He released her, and she got up and took her bag into the bathroom. She had chosen her clothes with care, washed her hair the night before, shaved her legs, put on lightly scented skin lotion—and he had wanted her when she was sweaty and sandy, with her hair damp and tangled. Not very romantic.

She showered quickly and put on her nightgown. It wasn't fancy, but she looked nice in it. She had gotten a little color in spite of the sunscreen. She rubbed lotion on her arms and put a touch behind her ears—locking the barn door. When she came out, Frank was wearing one of the hotel's white terry bathrobes. He had closed the drapes, turned on the electric fireplace, and turned down his bed. "Oh, I like that," he said, coming to meet her. He put his arms around her and said, "You smell good."

"Lavender," she explained. She reached inside the robe to rub his shoulders. She was feeling something new now, something tender, loving, intimate, possessive. She kissed him. She wanted to give in to this sense of well-being, of the inevitability of a future together, of love, but wasn't it too soon?

"Teresa," he said, again as if her name was a special endearment. "I want to sleep with you. I want to hold you all night."

"It sounds very romantic," she said, "but what if I snore? What if I need you to let me breathe a little?"

"Breathing is overrated. I never want to let go of you again." He kissed her, and then he lifted her in his arms. It had never happened to her before—Gene hadn't even carried her across the threshold on their wedding night.

"Frank!" she cried, laughing, but a little scared—what if he dropped her? He was strong, but she wasn't very light. He didn't drop her—or he did, but deliberately, from about an inch above the cool, clean sheets of his bed. They were both laughing, and he started kissing her randomly, here and there. This can be a lot of fun, she told herself. Enjoy it while it lasts. "Remember when you asked if it was too soon for me to date?" she asked.

"Yeah, and you said it depended on the definition."

"It turns out it *was* too soon," she said, "and now it's too late."

"Uh-huh," he said, as if it made sense to him. "But sometimes things just happen." He kissed her again and slid his hand up her thigh, under her nightgown.

Teresa remembered she was a responsible adult. "We need to use protection this time," she insisted.

"Are you sure?" he asked. His hand kept moving up, and he kissed her shoulder. "You have a son, but every woman wants a daughter. I'd love to make a little girl with you."

"That's crazy," she said. "We barely know each other, and I'm not even going to think about having another baby unless I'm married."

"Let's get married, then."

"Frank!" She laughed, but she wasn't sure he wasn't serious. "You want to marry me so you don't have to use a condom?"

"No, I want to marry you because I don't ever want this to end."

"But this isn't marriage, Frank. Marriage is loading the dishwasher and bandaging skinned knees and leaving the top off the toothpaste."

"I never do that."

"Me either, but—"

"See? We're very compatible, and besides I'm crazy about you. I knew the first time I saw you. We can take it slow if you have doubts, but I don't have any."

"Well, you should. How many other women have you wanted to marry?"

"One," he said. "No, two. The one I married and Jennifer Lopez."

Teresa threw a pillow at him.

Chapter 8

She never slept well in a strange bed, but she was comfortable enough, and the sound of the surf helped. She was only half asleep when Frank got out of bed to take a shower, but she didn't move until he came back and bent to kiss her. "Time to get up, sleepyhead. Get dressed, and we'll go out to breakfast."

She stretched and sat up. He drew back the drapes, letting in the sunlight and the ocean view. It looked like it would be another beautiful day. He was dressed in jeans and a navy blue polo shirt.

"Wear the shirt I bought for you yesterday," he said as she picked up her overnight bag.

"Okay—where is it?" She looked around.

"Oh, I guess I left them in the car," he said. "I'll go out and get it."

"No, Frank, I'll wear something else," she said, but he took his key card and headed on out the door. She shrugged and went into the bathroom. She washed up, brushed her teeth, and dressed in jeans. He tapped on the door, and she opened it wide enough to take the T-shirt. She snipped the tag off with her fingernail scissors and looked at the label. It was a size smaller than she would have chosen—she liked them loose for comfort—and she didn't usually wear the V-neck style, but it was pretty, and she thought it would fit.

It did, if a little snugly, and she loved the color and

the sea anemone design. It showed where they had been and what she liked—a definite plus for self-expression. Frank smiled when she emerged from the bathroom. "I knew it would look great on you," he said, and then he held up the handcuffs.

"Why did you bring those in?" she asked. Police work wasn't supposed to intrude on their holiday. In answer, he took her hand and closed one of the cuffs around her wrist. "What the hell, Frank?"

"You are under arrest," he said. She was too stunned to resist when he put the other one on. "For grand theft, heart," he added. He was smiling, but it didn't feel like a joke to her. She was not amused.

"Take them off," she said.

"You have the right to remain compliant," he said.

"Very funny. Now take them off."

"You said you liked handcuffs," he said. "Remember?"

"This isn't what I meant. Take them off right now."

"Okay, okay." He found the key in his pocket and unlocked the cuffs. "I didn't mean to make you uncomfortable. I guess we should have talked about it first."

"Talked about what?" She rubbed her wrists. Her heart was beating too fast.

"I thought it might be fun to try something a little different."

"Like role-playing, you mean? I'm not playing that role. I'm a little claustrophobic. I did not like it." She spoke as emphatically as she could without raising her voice.

"Sorry," he said and kissed her consolingly. "I shouldn't have surprised you. Let's eat, and we can talk about it later."

She couldn't think of anything to say. What had she gotten herself into now? She put on her shoes and picked up her purse while he told her where they were going—the hotel's Beachfront Grill, the source of last night's wonderful burgers. She said nothing as they headed down the stairs and across the parking lot. It was sunny but still cool, and she hadn't brought her sweater. "Are you mad at me?" Frank asked.

"No, I just...I don't know what to say."

He took her hand and squeezed it. "I'm sorry." He sounded very contrite. "Are you really claustrophobic?"

"A little."

"Obviously I didn't know. Like elevators and—?"

"No, or only if I was trapped in one."

They were at the entrance to the restaurant by then, and he opened the door for her. The large room offered a panoramic view of the ocean, and they were seated right away at a table next to one of the many picture windows. Like most restaurants in the coastal towns, this one specialized in seafood, but the breakfast menu offered plenty of variety, and the prices were very reasonable.

"What sounds good?" Frank asked her.

Teresa decided to be reckless. "I think I'll have Bananas Foster French toast."

"I'd like more protein," he said.

"I love breakfast."

"Me too." He grinned. "Most important meal of the day." He ordered a three-egg scramble with country fried potatoes. Teresa kept her gaze on the lovely view, but she was remembering linguini at the Perfect Place and the first-date awkwardness of not knowing what to say. Now they had been physically intimate, and she still didn't know him. She wanted to go home.

"Teresa, please don't be mad."

"I'm not. It's so beautiful out there." She looked at him. His eyes were dark, filled with concern for her. Tall, dark, and handsome—every little girl's dream.

"I didn't mean to spoil the mood," he said. "We can't discuss it here, but the last thing I meant to do was upset you."

"It's all right. Let's just enjoy our breakfast and the view. This is good coffee, isn't it?" She took another sip. She usually avoided too much caffeine, but it would be a long day. She looked out at the waves and remembered what she was thinking before he spoke. "I don't even know your full name," she said.

"That's an easy one. Francis Prescott McAllister."

"Prescott?"

"Yeah, we were supposedly descendants of William Prescott, who was some kind of Revolutionary War hero. It turned out it wasn't true, but I was stuck with the name."

"I like it."

"What's yours?"

"My maiden name was Maria Teresa Seguin."

"Ah, my little Latina!"

"Only half."

"You speak Spanish?"

"Only what I learned in high school, and I've forgotten a lot of it. *Olvidé mas que recuerdo.* My best line is *Creo que su inglés es mejor que mi español.*"

He didn't ask her to translate. "So Lansing is your married name? You kept the jerk's name?"

"It's easier when you have kids—to have the same

76

name."

"Would you change it if you got married again?"

"Maybe, but I wasn't planning to."

"But you are now." He reached out and gave her hand a quick squeeze.

"No, I'm not."

"Yes, you are." He said it teasingly, but she still didn't like it. "Think about it—if we were married, I could put you on my insurance, and we could do the cochlear implant." He could see she was about to protest and held up a hand. "I know you think he's perfect, and I'm not trying to fix him."

"Frank! Slow down!"

"When is Oktoberfest? I want to meet your boy."

"Next weekend, and his name is Aiden."

"Right. I know you and *Aiden* are a package deal, and I promise I'll do my best to develop a good relationship with him."

She took a deep breath. "I should teach you a few signs."

"Yeah, okay. Does he read lips?"

"Yes, but it's hard work, especially with new people—a lot of guesswork." She fingerspelled h-i. "You can use that for hi. Or this." She made the sign for hello.

He didn't try to imitate her. "Let's not do it here."

"If signing in public embarrasses you—"

"No, but I feel stupid because I don't know any yet. You can teach me later. Oktoberfest is the whole weekend? We'll go Saturday morning, then." He wasn't asking; he was telling her.

"Frank!" She was alarmed by how easily he could take control of her life, but it was as if she had been in freefall for a while, and now she had landed—safely? Or in a hostile wilderness?

"What?"

"Nothing—go on."

"What do they have to eat? Anything good?"

"A few things—German potato salad, sauerbraten, Black Forest cake. Aiden will want hot dogs."

"Is there a sign for that?"

She showed him. He nodded, but he didn't try it. Still, he had asked. It was a start.

****

Walking back to the room, they held hands, and there was a sense of belonging they hadn't had before. It was something she had been missing for a while without realizing it. A woman did not need a man to be complete, but raising a child as a single parent could be a very lonely struggle.

Teresa went into the bathroom and brushed her teeth, and when she came out, Frank was sitting on his bed and gestured for her to join him. When she did he took her hand and held it in both of his. The handcuffs were on the nightstand, and he nodded toward them. "I'm sorry I sprung those on you, but…you seemed so open, and I thought you'd like it."

"I didn't."

"I know. No bullshit between us. You can always tell me how you feel. It's not a big deal either way, but let me explain what I have in mind."

"Not if it involves handcuffs."

"No, I can see the handcuffs were a bad idea. The claustrophobia comes from not being able to get free, right? You're okay in an elevator because you know the door will open?"

"I guess so."

"Now if I took the belt from this robe"—the white terry hotel robe lay across the foot of the bed—"and tied your hands with it—"

"Which is *not* going to happen."

"It's soft and has a lot of give. If it was tied loosely, you could easily get free if you wanted to."

"No."

"The way it was explained to me is when you give up control, you don't have to take any responsibility, and you can relax and just enjoy whatever happens."

"Count me out. I'm not going to do it."

"I'm not talking about dominance and discipline. This isn't that at all. You know I would never hurt you, Teresa. I love you. This would be the simplest form of bondage, very light bondage. Lots of people do it."

"No, Frank. This is not for me, and it never will be. If you want bondage games, you have the wrong girl. Maybe Lacey will play with you." She couldn't keep the tinge of bitterness out of her voice.

"Who?"

"Lacey Norman. Waitress at the Cougar Grill? She—"

"Oh, the kind of slutty one?"

"Young, blonde, well-endowed. I didn't think she was slutty until she slept with Brett."

"You're kidding. He slept with *her*? It would be like gorging on Twinkies when you have fine Belgian chocolate at home." She didn't rise to the compliment, and he said, "So it's a no?"

"It's a no." She suspected it was also the end of this little romance—if it had ever been one.

"Okay," he said. "It's okay." He released her hand

and pulled her toward him for a quick, gentle kiss.

"Did your wife let you do those things?" She thought the discussion was finished now, and she was just curious.

"Yes. She liked it. In fact she was the one who got me into it."

"So it wasn't like a deep-seated preference of yours, just something you got into with her?"

"Right. Like I said, no big deal either way. Forget I asked." He kissed her temple and then let her go. "We don't have to check out until noon. Do you want to head back to the beach for a while, or go on to Bedford Light?"

"The lighthouse," she said. They had supposedly settled the matter, but she didn't particularly want to be in a hotel room with him right now.

They loaded the car and walked across the lot to the hotel desk. While Frank took care of the bill, Teresa ran her eyes over the headlines of the *Powell City Register* lying on the counter. A familiar name caught her attention—*Linedecker.* She picked up the paper. The third body found under the riverbank at Big Devil Creek had been identified. The name was being withheld pending notification of next of kin, but the victim was a young woman who had disappeared from Yaholo several months before. In the damp of the riverbed, her partially clad body had decomposed quickly. No traces of DNA were found to link to a suspect, but it was believed she had been sexually assaulted and strangled—while Wade Linedecker was safely locked up in state prison.

The hair on the back of Teresa's neck stood up. Yaholo was not much bigger than Cougar and about the same distance from Powell City. Small towns like Cougar might not be as safe as she had assumed. She remembered Frank saying Chelsea shouldn't bicycle home alone after dark. He was just being a cop, but maybe he was right.

She pointed the item out to him. "So Linedecker was telling the truth," he said.

"It's odd that somebody else would choose the same place to bury a murder victim. A copycat?"

"It was before he revealed where he'd buried his. It might be somebody who knew him, somebody he told. I imagine they'll look at his former cellmates and other associates."

Chapter 9

The weather stayed nearly perfect as the day went on. Frank and Teresa visited Bedford Light, which catered less to tourists than Oxhead and was more authentic to its historic origins, and drove on to Guardian Bay. It was a small but lively town with a quaint little harbor full of fishing boats, a whale watching station, several good restaurants, and dozens of gift shops where a wide range of souvenirs could be bought. One store was completely devoted to kites, which Aiden would like, and numerous shops offered everything from jewelry to sunglasses.

Teresa had her hands full keeping a lid on Frank's desire to buy her everything she showed an interest in. She wondered if he was trying to make up to her for the earlier unpleasantness. They did buy saltwater taffy for Aiden and Sasha and fudge for Alix and spent considerable time in the largest T-shirt shop, where any of a wide variety of designs could be heat-transferred onto the shirt of the buyer's choice. He bought a white crew neck with a picture of the Guardian Bridge for himself, and when she couldn't immediately choose which of two she wanted, he bought them both. She had the lighthouse design put on a long-sleeved navy blue shirt and an intricate flower pattern on pink.

They ate lunch at Tavier's, a quiet, charming family restaurant with a view of the harbor.

Considering what she'd had for breakfast, she wanted something light and settled for a salmon-and-cucumber salad while he ordered a steak sandwich. Tavier's had no children's menu, so they crossed it off the list of possible places to take Aiden. She was emotionally exhausted and a bit tired of eating out, but she did her best to enjoy herself.

After lunch, they stood for a while at the sea wall, soaking in the sun and the view. Frank suggested a whale watching expedition, but Teresa was ready to go home. "Okay," he said, "but I'd like to make one stop on the way."

This proved to be a shopping center where Frank took her to a store called Cellphone Source. "This is too much!" Teresa protested.

"I'll feel better if you have a decent phone for emergencies," he said. He asked her a few questions about her preferences, but ignored all of her objections. He bought her a state-of-the-art smartphone with a lot more features than she would ever need and a smaller, simpler phone for Aiden. "I know you'll have to set limits for him," he said, "but he can use it to text you."

"He's six years old!"

"Does the little girl he plays with have one?"

"Yes, but I don't think it's anything fancy. I think she's too young, but Alix said kids are smarter than we are about them and she might as well have one."

"Good argument. It will be a great way for them to communicate and help with their reading skills. "

"If we want them to learn text-speak."

"It's a way he can fit in better with other kids, too—he can text them if they don't know sign language."

"I think it's too much for a boy his age, and this one is way too fancy for me. I won't be able to figure out how to use it."

"Yes, you will. I'll get it set up for you, and it will be a cinch. Are you sure this is the color you want?"

"Frank, I really don't think this is a good idea."

"It's a great idea, and you know it."

She gave in, but a little later, as they drove back into familiar territory, she thought, Wait, what just happened? This isn't me. This isn't the person I am. The entire weekend had been like a dream in which she struggled to control events and kept failing. She decided she would work out how to make herself clear to Frank and give the phones back in the next few days.

He insisted on carrying her overnight bag and most of her packages into the house. He'd had only a quick look at the living room when he paid Chelsea the week before, and she couldn't say no when he asked for a tour. "This place come furnished?" he asked.

"No, just the appliances. The rest is mine, mostly things my parents gave me when they moved to the city."

He admired the paintings she had hung—one of bamboo and chrysanthemums and one of fishing boats—and commented on the size of the television set. "I guess I'm used to my big screen," he said.

"It's big enough for us," Teresa said. "And it has closed captioning."

"No computer? These days—"

"I know, I know."

In the kitchen, he asked, "You actually cook on this old thing?" of the stove and, sensing her defensiveness, quickly added, "I like the curtains."

She tried to make quick work of the bedrooms, a perfunctory look at Aiden's, small and cluttered, and matter-of-factly, "This is mine," standing in the doorway.

"Where did you get the bed?" he asked.

"My parents gave it to me—it belonged to my grandparents."

"It looks like a real antique. I love old mission-style furniture."

"Me too." Something else they had in common.

"I like what you've done with the place," he said after he'd seen everything. "Do you have a lease or is it month to month?"

Exasperated, she stood her ground. "I know why you're asking. Stop rushing things. I'll be here a long while yet, no matter what happens between us. We need to take this one step at a time." As if they hadn't already skipped a few.

"Fair enough," he said. He kissed her quickly. "I'll call you tomorrow."

As soon as he was gone, she got into the pickup and drove to Alix's. Aiden didn't run out this time. Alix's car wasn't in the driveway, and she didn't recognize the one parked in front of the house. She was earlier than she had predicted and hoped they weren't out somewhere. She looked at her watch. Alix would be at the grill—Sunday was not a day when she was likely to leave her staff on their own—but she had promised not to park Aiden there the whole time.

She knocked and immediately heard running feet. Sasha opened the door. "What did you bring me?" she asked.

"That's a fine greeting!" Teresa said.

Sasha giggled. "Hi," she said. "What did you bring me?"

"I brought you some saltwater taffy."

"Yay!" She ran into the living room, and Teresa followed more slowly. At the dining room table, Aiden sat dispiritedly in a chair with playing cards in his hand. He looked up and immediately dropped the cards and threw himself at her, wrapping his arms tight around her waist. She ruffled his hair and looked up again at the table.

On the far side, seated calmly with her cards spread in a pretty, precise fan, was Lacey Norman.

"You've got to be kidding," was all Teresa could say.

Lacey laughed and stood up. "Hello, Terry," she said.

"Don't call me Terry." She wanted to say, Why are *you* here, you skuzzy whore? She settled for, "Don't you have a job?"

Lacey laughed again. "Don't worry. Alix asked me to drop them off, but your babysitter is on the way."

Teresa dug out her new phone. Frank had set it up so she was able to tap Chelsea's name on her frequent calls list. There was a brief wait while she hoped Chelsea was steering her bicycle off the road. "I'm home," she said. "Sorry for the false alarm. I'll pay you extra next time."

"Okay," Chelsea said cheerfully. "No problem."

Teresa hung up. "Why are you still here?" she asked Lacey.

"Why are you such a bitch?" Lacey asked coolly. She tossed her cards on the table, picked up her purse, and left. "'Bye, kids," she called at the door.

"Lacey said bitch," Sasha signed. She signed it to Aiden, but he wasn't looking.

"Mama," he said plaintively, looking up tearfully at her. "No more trip."

"No," she agreed. "No more trips without you. I missed you so much!" He clung so fiercely she couldn't help feeling terribly guilty. Sasha tugged at his arm and signed, "Candy."

"Yes, I brought you some saltwater taffy." She fingerspelled t-a-f-f-y to be sure he understood—she didn't know a sign for it.

He let go of her and signed, "Go home?"

"Yes, we'll go home now. Do you want to come with us and spend the night, Sasha? I can take you back to the grill if you want."

"I'll go with you," she said eagerly. She gathered up the playing cards and ran into her bedroom.

"Sasha kicks," Aiden said. He signed, "In bed."

"We'll go home and sleep in our own beds," she said. "Sasha can have the couch. Thank you for saying good night to me last night. It made me feel better. Did you have a good time?" He nodded, but reluctantly. "What did you do?"

"We play games," he signed. "Go to park. Swings." He brightened. "Chuck E. Cheese," he said aloud.

Sasha returned with her backpack. "Did you get your toothbrush?" Teresa asked. "Clean underwear?" Sasha nodded. She was a good little traveler.

In the pickup, Aiden was more relaxed, and he and Sasha filled her in on the details of their weekend. Teresa wanted to hear every word, but underneath she seethed with anger. How could Alix leave her child with Lacey, of all people, even briefly? She didn't expect Alix to fire the girl—she was a decent waitress, and the customers liked her—but this was too much. She also thought Aiden was holding something back. Something was making him unhappy. Maybe he was angry with her for leaving him.

She *was* glad to sleep in her own bed. *Be it ever so humble...* She thought about Frank with a certain wariness at first, and then she let herself remember the pleasure...

Chapter 10

Monday morning's *Independent* had the name of the Yaholo woman who had been buried on the bank of Big Devil Creek. She was reported missing by her concerned family, certain she was the victim of foul play, but her friends told the police she might have left town voluntarily with the new man in her life. She was an adult, and there was no evidence to go on, so not much had been done to find her. With Wade Linedecker eliminated by the timing, there were no immediate suspects in her murder.

"I *am* sorry," Alix said, over coffee in Teresa's kitchen after the children had been delivered to school. "It seemed like a good idea at the time, and I thought what you didn't know wouldn't hurt you. You know, Lacey's not a bad person. It's not like she would corrupt our kids. She just gave them a ride and played a game of Crazy Eights with them."

"She raises her voice when she talks to Aiden," Teresa said. "I hate that." She knew she was being petty. It wasn't as if Lacey was a predatory seductress. It took two to tango.

"She means well," Alix said vaguely. "While I'm apologizing, I should tell you something else you won't like—if Aiden didn't tell you?"

She shook her head. He *was* holding something back, after all.

"Brett came by. I know you don't want him to see him, but maybe it was a good thing—"

"You let him talk to Aiden?" Her anger rose again. "Whose side are you on?"

"Yours, of course. He told me not to tell you, but I thought you should know. He was only there for a few minutes, and I wouldn't let him talk to him alone, and I think all he wanted was to say he was sorry and missed him. Maybe it's better if Aiden doesn't feel like he abandoned him completely."

She shook her head. "It made him sad, and if it raised his hopes—"

"Well, you know, Terror, a lot of couples can get past infidelity issues."

"You *are* on his side."

"No, I'm on yours. Always. I'm just saying. You know, kids can blame themselves for a breakup, so I think it's better if he knows Brett wishes they could still be friends."

"Which puts all the blame on me."

"No, it doesn't, and he didn't say anything against you. I know we don't always see eye to eye on child-raising, but I won't do anything against your wishes." She sipped her coffee and looked at Teresa. "Anything more, I mean." She shrugged. "It's not like I asked him to come. I just didn't see the harm."

"I think he's the one who should apologize to both of us. He put you on the spot, and it was really sneaky to try to do it behind my back."

Alix patted her hand. "Thanks, Terror. I knew you would understand. Now tell me about your weekend!"

"It was good."

"Good as in okay or good as in everything you

always wanted out of life?"

"Somewhere in between."

"Uh-huh. So…you shaved your legs, didn't you?"

"We went to the beach. I wore my shorts."

"Oh, you did it, didn't you? Yeah, I can tell. Oh, Terror! Well, good for you—you could use a little liberation."

"I'm as liberated as the next girl."

"Yeah, right. So…was he good?"

"You know I'm not going to answer that," Teresa said. She looked into her steaming coffee cup. "Yes." She felt herself blush.

"Yes?" Alix asked eagerly.

"Yes. End of discussion."

"Details, details!"

"No details, but…Best. Foreplay. Ever."

"Really?" Alix asked enviously. "He looked like he'd be in a hurry."

"He is kind of trying to rush the relationship. He asked me to marry him."

"He did not! Was he joking?"

"It was hard to tell. Probably. But he—well, maybe it's just me. It's like he's ready to take charge of my entire life. Maybe I've been too independent for too long. I was the same way with Brett—maybe that's why he wanted out. Maybe I pushed him away." It was tempting to blame herself or Lacey and forgive Brett, but the hurt ran too deep, and now she had moved on.

"Don't start blaming yourself. Brett was a very bad boy. Anyway, like I told you before, you have to *tell* Frank if he's going too fast for you. You know rushing things is one of the signs of an abuser."

"He certainly isn't abusive, physically or verbally.

He treats me like a queen. It would be nice to think he actually fell in love with me at first sight—why is that so hard for me to believe?"

"Low self-esteem?"

"As in I don't deserve such a hot guy, et cetera, et cetera? Maybe."

"Frank *is* a catch. Good-looking, sexy, has a good job—"

"A dangerous job."

"For which he is paid handsomely. He could afford to keep you in a style to which I would love to see you become accustomed. He's perfect."

Teresa looked into her coffee cup again. "Pretty nearly," she said, but she had waited too long.

"What?" Alix was entirely too eager.

She was sure the bondage suggestion was in the category of private things that should remain between her and Frank, but she was so used to talking to Alix about whatever troubled her. "He wanted to tie me up," she confessed.

Alix stared at her. "Oh. My. God. Did you let him?"

"No, of course not."

"Oh, yeah, what was he thinking? Nice church-going, small-town girl like you?"

"I'm not a prude. Between consenting adults—you know, whatever floats your boat. But *I* don't want to do it."

"Yeah, okay." Alix considered. "Might be fun," she said. "I mean I might go for it with a hot guy like that."

"I thought you were through with men."

"Yeah," she said regretfully. "They do come with a

few drawbacks. Fun to dream, though. If you decide you don't want him…"

Teresa laughed. As usual, Alix had made her feel better. "Let me show you what we bought. Or what Frank bought. All I got was postcards and a stupid coffee mug for him." She brought out the packages and gave Alix the fudge and saltwater taffy. "I let the kids have one piece last night," she said. "I know Sasha prefers the licorice, but we can do half of each if you want. The fudge is for my very best friend, of course."

"My favorite! Thank you!"

"He bought these shirts for Aiden—this one changes color in the sun—and a silly stuffed fish, which he loved. That kid is so easy! I got these two shirts at a place where you have them made to order while you wait. I would have bought you one, but I know you never wear them." She held up the T-shirts.

"Nice. And Frank paid for all this?"

"Yes, and he picked one out—oh, it's in the laundry. Let me get it." She went out and returned with the light blue V-neck.

"Pretty color," Alix said. "What are those nasty things?"

"They're sea anemones, and I think they're beautiful. Alix, he noticed I liked them best—I didn't say anything."

"Cops are trained to be observant."

"It's a little tight, but—"

"It's cute. No, what it is is sexy. He probably wanted it tight. You know what this means—he doesn't mind you looking sexy. He won't be super jealous when other guys look at you. I like that in a man."

"Oh, and this." She held up the blue bracelet. "It's

not diamonds, but I like it, and he was so sweet about it."

"You are *so* lucky." Alix sighed. Teresa *did* feel lucky now—was it Frank, or was it her friend's approval?

"Yeah—and oh, I haven't shown you the—I'm not sure if it's the best or the worst part." She retrieved her purse and showed her the smartphone. "He got a phone for Aiden, too. I didn't give it to him yet, but Frank said it would be good because he could text me instead of depending on somebody else to relay on the phone."

"Good idea," Alix approved. "Wow, Teresa, this is some phone. You know you can do e-mail and internet on it too."

"Not if I don't pay for a service provider."

"Yes, you can. Look—it has 4G. He must have paid for the plan, too."

"I can't let him do this—can I?"

"I would."

"He kept saying I wasn't obligated and he knew I couldn't be bought, he likes to spend money to make people happy, and so on."

"He just gets better and better. High five, girl, you scored!" She held up her hand, and Teresa complied halfheartedly. She wasn't sure what she had scored. "You know what we should do? We should Google him. If you're worried he's scamming you or something."

"I don't want to snoop behind his back."

"Yes, you do. I hate to use the internet on these tiny screens, but it sure is handy to always have it with you."

"Instead of calling you."

"Nah, I like being your personal reference librarian, but this will have its uses. Okay—McAllister? M C or Mac? Way too many hits. Doctor—no—CEO of Stillwater Mining Company—blah, blah, blah. Is he Francis or Franklin or just Frank?"

"Francis Prescott."

"Classy. Prescott is a Bush family name; maybe he's related. No, no hits."

"Try his name and Powell City and SWAT."

Alix thumbed buttons. "Here we go. Two articles in the *Powell City Register*—SWAT Officer Frank McAllister, 33—quoted as saying, blah, blah—this was last year—ooh, he shot somebody."

The knowledge gave Teresa a chill feeling, but she said calmly, "It's what they do—when they have to. Let me see."

Alix was right; reading the article on the tiny screen was not ideal. He had been placed on administrative leave—which was routine with officer-involved shootings—after an armed robber was critically injured during an exchange of gunfire. She took a deep breath. At least the robber wasn't killed. She wondered if he had ever killed anybody. She handed the phone back. "Could we find his wife's obituary?" she asked, feeling a little guilty.

"Probably. Do you know her name?"

"No."

"Too many hits…Okay—how about this— 'husband Frank McAllister' and 'Powell City' and 'obituary'—yup, six hits."

"It would have been a while ago—he's sort of over it."

"How about this one? Edris Quentin McAllister of

Genoa—Edris, really? Yuck! Survived by her husband Frank McAllister. It's very brief. Died at home. Somebody told me that was obituary speak for suicide."

"He said it was an accident. Most accidents happen at home."

"Yeah, maybe she accidentally slit her wrists. The other ones—'preceded in death by her husband'—this one was eighty-nine. Edris was thirty-six three years ago, so older than him? Like five years?"

It made sense to Teresa—a woman introducing her younger husband to a new sexual practice. And he had lived in Genoa, which explained his familiarity with the coast. It was strange that he hadn't said so—and why hadn't she asked? "Look up Edris Quentin. Maybe there's more."

Alix complied. "No—they're all Edris comma Quentin. Edris McAllister?" She thumbed keys. "Really? That many? Can't tell if any are her—no good info anyway. Wait—here it is. Coroner's inquest— Edris McAllister of Genoa, death by accident or misadventure. So I guess she didn't slit her wrists."

"What else does it say?" Teresa asked with some trepidation. She wasn't sure she wanted any details Frank didn't choose to share with her.

"Nada. Just the one line in a court proceedings list."

She took the phone back and sipped her coffee. "I'm sorry we looked," she said.

"Knowledge is power, kiddo."

Teresa shook her head. She didn't want to know Frank's wife was older than he was, with an odd name like Edris, and dead at thirty-six. She didn't want to know Edris had given him a taste for bondage. She didn't want to know she had used his generous gift to check on him.

****

He called her at work in the evening, his voice warm and familiar. "I've been thinking about you all day," he said. "Are you busy?"

"Yes, but I can talk for a few minutes. What were you thinking about me?" She thought she could guess, but she was wrong.

"I wanted to see you smile. Your whole face lights up when you smile. And you have this slightly crooked tooth—"

"So you were thinking about my imperfections?"

"It's very cute. You have no idea how beautiful you are."

"Really, Frank, when you lay it on so thick, I start to wonder what you're trying to sell me. The Brooklyn Bridge?"

"See? You don't have a clue. I can't wait until Saturday to see you. When can we get together?"

"The weekend was very hard on Aiden. I can't leave him alone again so soon."

"Okay, so it has to be when he's in school. Lunch? You get a lunch hour, don't you?"

"Yes. I usually bring a sack lunch. Aren't you working in Powell City?"

"Yes. Tomorrow—no. Wednesday. I could do Wednesday. I could pick you up at work, and we could have lunch at my place."

"Or at the grill or the Spicy Burger on the highway," she said, "since it's my beautiful smile you want to see. I can smile at the Spicy Burger."

He laughed, a rich, warm, real laugh. He liked her.

97

It was exactly the same feeling she had had in junior high school when Bobby Zaragoza carried her books— *He likes me; a boy likes me.* "Okay," Frank said. "Spicy Burger."

****

"I didn't expect it to be so easy," she told Alix on the phone.

"You thought he wanted a little afternoon delight? You should go to his place sometime soon, though, before you get in too deep."

"I am in too deep."

"Any deeper, then. You can learn a lot about a man from his bachelor pad. Stuff about what he'd be like to live with. It's good he wants you to see it—means he's not married."

"I wasn't worried about that."

"You should have been. It happens all the time. Are you afraid he'll tie you up?"

"No, I think I made myself clear. It does creep me out a little, though. His wanting it, I mean. He said something about liking my vulnerability—maybe he thought I would be an easy mark."

"Were you?'

"Not as easy as he expected, but…maybe I am. What I keep thinking is…he'll take care of me. It would be so easy to let him. Stop struggling. Stop going it alone, chin up, stiff upper lip."

"Yeah," Alix said. "Tempting."

"I don't want to depend on him. I can't. After Brett, I can't depend on anybody. It's too soon…I don't know what I was thinking."

"He's too damn hot to pass up?"

Teresa laughed. "Yeah, there's that."

Chapter 11

On Wednesday she made herself a lunch as she always did, in case Frank had to cancel and leave her to her own devices. Life with a SWAT officer would require a lot of flexibility. Her caution seemed justified when he called to say he was running late and couldn't pick her up. He wanted her to meet him at the Spicy Burger instead. He was very apologetic, and the request was perfectly reasonable, but a niggling part of her mind wondered if he didn't want to call attention to their relationship by being seen at her workplace.

He wasn't at the Spicy Burger when she arrived, but she had barely climbed out of the pickup when his Acura pulled into the lot. He parked close, got out, and headed straight toward her, smiling eagerly. He took hold of her shoulders and kissed her hard. "God, I missed you," he said.

"I guess you did," she said dryly. She wasn't used to PDA—Brett would never do more than hold hands in public, which might be why Frank had assumed they were married.

"It was a rough morning," he said. "I'm so ready for this."

"Did somebody get hurt?"

"No, but it was touch and go for a while." He put his arm around her as they headed toward the entrance.

"Did you ever get shot?" she asked.

"No. Somebody hit me with a bottle once. I have a scar, but you can't see it." He touched his head just above the hairline. "How was *your* morning?"

"Pretty routine."

"You shouldn't have to waste your time on such a dead-end job," he said.

"I like it."

"But what you really want is to be a veterinarian, right? You could be a full-time mom and finish college online."

"And live on what?"

"Hm, let me see…." He was teasing her.

"I see. I suppose you'd want me barefoot and pregnant?"

"Well, you do have pretty toes. Think how great it would be for your son. I'm sure you're doing the best you can, but he needs a strong male role model and a mother who can devote all her time to him."

Teresa repressed everything she would have liked to say and let him open the door for her. The Spicy Burger was busy, and they were in line long enough for him to put his arms around her from behind, press her against him, and touch her breasts in a way she found very disturbing. She couldn't decide whether it was a good kind of disturbing or a bad kind.

"Frank…" They were in a public place, after all.

"Damn!" he said. She didn't have to ask what he meant. She was feeling the same way. He kissed her ear and nuzzled her cheek. "What do you want to eat?" he asked blandly, pretending nothing was happening between them. When it was their turn, he ordered two jumbo burgers with cheese and no onion.

"For here or to go?" the clerk asked.

"Teresa?" Frank said in the caressing way that made her name sound like an endearment. His hands distracted her, and she couldn't answer fast enough. "To go," he said.

Apartment buildings in Cougar were scarce, so she was not surprised Frank's place was in the recent development at the end of River Road. It was a new building with four large units, and his apartment was very modern and masculine, to her taste almost sterile, but with clean lines, beautiful furniture, and hardwood floors. It bore no feminine touches, no pictures of Edris, no sign any woman had ever lived in it. At first she saw only the living room and the bedroom. "The food will get cold," she protested, but without much conviction.

"That's why they make microwaves," he said.

The bed was king-sized and very comfortable. She lay back against soft, silk-encased pillows, and he kissed her until she couldn't breathe. "You are so damn hot," he said, sliding his hands under her T-shirt, inside her bra.

"It's not me," she said. "Adrenaline probably makes you horny."

"No, it's definitely you. You know how in the movies they always show people tearing each other's clothes off?"

"Hollywood sex," she said dismissively.

"I never wanted to do that until I laid eyes on you."

"Yeah, well, I have to go back to work, so you'd better not tear anything."

He laughed, delighted. "You are a breath of fresh air, Teresa. I want to make a baby with you."

"No, Frank. Get a condom or we're not doing this. We're not teenagers."

"What did I say about you not being tough?" he asked. He kissed her. "Let wiser heads prevail."

****

The microwave was large and stainless steel, like the stove, refrigerator, and sink. The countertops were black granite, the backsplash glass tile, and the cabinets white maple and glass. The spouting whale mug she had given him was next to the coffeemaker. Frank tried to separate the tomato, lettuce, and pickles from the burgers, in order to reheat them, and made a mess of it. Teresa took over.

"Obviously I need a wife," he said. "This place has two bedrooms. If we got married—"

"Patience is a virtue, Frank."

"One I don't have, where you're concerned."

When the burgers were ready, they sat at the kitchen table to eat. "Okay, here it comes," Teresa said. "I'm going to make a speech, like a damned Hallmark movie."

"Uh-oh," he said, but he didn't sound worried.

"You know this will pass," she said. "This honeymoon phase. New love. Then you have to face reality. You have a dangerous, high-stress career, and I have a child with a disability and abandonment issues. I'm too independent to be the kind of wife you need, and you seem to want to smother me. My life is a struggle right now, and it would be so tempting to let you rescue me, but we'd both be sorry in the end. I've taken too much from you already. I need to give you back the phones. I don't even know what the charges will be."

"The bill will come to me. Don't worry about it."

"I can't let you do that! A gift is one thing, but

paying my bills is—"

"Teresa."

"What?"

"That's all bullshit." He reached across the table to take her hand. "This is real. And you know what? Hallmark movies always have happy endings. I'm totally sympathetic with the whole women's lib thing, but you need help, and I can—"

"You're going too fast! We have to take it slow. You haven't even met Aiden."

"Let's do it, then. I love you, and I'm proud of it. I'm tired of sneaking around trying to keep this secret. Can I stop by tonight?"

"No, you can't. We have to take it one step at a time and start with a brief meeting on neutral ground."

"You know best when it concerns your son, of course," he said, "but I think you'll see I'm right about this. It seems so…inevitable to me."

"If it is, waiting won't change it."

"All right." He took a deep breath. "Show me those signs again."

When the brief lesson was over, she told him about Alix letting Brett see Aiden. "She thinks he should know Brett didn't want to abandon him."

Frank shook his head. "He shouldn't try to be friends with a man who hurt his mother. I hope you know I would never do that."

She should have said yes, but she took a big bite out of her burger and said nothing.

"Teresa?" He took her hand again, but she wouldn't meet his eyes. "Oh, I know what this is," he said regretfully. "I shouldn't have brought up the bondage thing. Please forget about it. I wouldn't have hurt you, but if I scared you or made you think I'm a pervert—"

"You did make me uncomfortable," she said.

"I wouldn't even have thought of it if you hadn't said what you did about the handcuffs."

"I meant I liked them as a dramatic image. It wasn't about sex."

"I'm sorry. You didn't smile much after I brought it up, and I missed your smile. I'd still like to try it with you, but you know, you can't have everything. You'd probably like me to be George Clooney."

Teresa laughed. "No, but I wouldn't mind seeing Lake Como sometime. I'll tell you what—" She could joke about it now. "If you take me to Italy, you can tie me up."

"It's a deal."

****

"His apartment is bigger than my house," she told Alix on the phone. "It's not my style, but it's obviously expensive. I hate stainless steel, but the kitchen is beautiful. And the bathroom! Subway tile, huge glass-walled shower, jetted tub, double sinks."

"And did you see the bedroom?" Alix asked suggestively.

"Big walk-in closet."

"And—?"

"Silk sheets. Don't ask."

"So, it's going well?"

Teresa sighed. "I don't know. This is sort of lopsided. I like him, and the sex is great, but I don't feel like I'm falling in love, and he seems to be totally obsessed with me."

"You know, kiddo, you're probably still pretty

numb emotionally. My advice is to enjoy this for whatever it is—an exciting rebound fling—and see what develops down the road."

"Yeah, but things are developing a little too fast on his end."

"Repeat after me: Slow down, Frank."

"I've said it a hundred times."

"Keep saying it," Alix advised.

****

Thursday night, when she and Aiden came into the grill, Frank was sitting at the counter with a nearly empty beer mug in front of him. He was talking to Lacey, which gave her a pang, but the conversation looked casual enough. Alix was busy with a customer, and Teresa sent Aiden to sit in the corner booth.

"What are you doing?" she asked.

Frank looked around, pretending surprise. "Oh, hi, Teresa." Lacey sniffed and sashayed away. "Having a beer," he said blandly. "Fancy meeting you here." The twinkle in his eye told her it was no coincidence.

"How did you know I'd be here?"

"You mentioned it. Thursday, as usual." Had she? She didn't remember saying anything, but she hadn't been censoring herself with him. "We met here—on a Thursday."

"Right." It wasn't that she wasn't glad to see him—she had in fact felt a definite tingle of pleasure—but he was upsetting what they had planned. She shook her head at him, gave Alix a little wave, and joined her son.

She had just sat down and put her purse on the seat when Sasha ran up with a menu in hand, very fetching in an apron much too big for her. "What you gonna

105

have, missus?" she asked pertly.

Teresa laughed. "What would you recommend, miss?"

"Octopus," Sasha said. She giggled.

"Fried or grilled?"

"Fried with…strawberry sauce."

"I see. In that case, I think I'll have the meatloaf sandwich."

Sasha turned to Aiden. "What you gonna have, mister?"

He signed, "Hot dog, noodles, cheese."

"What was that, mister? Speak up, please. Golly shakes!"

"Don't tease, Sasha," Teresa said. Was Frank right? Did Sasha bully Aiden? Or was she overprotective? To Aiden she signed, "Say, 'Same as always.'"

He repeated the signs and said distinctly, if not very loudly, "The usual."

Sasha grinned and ran off to put in their orders. "Good job," Teresa said warmly.

She was sitting with her back to the bar—Aiden liked the far corner—but she was very much aware of Frank getting up and walking toward the booth. "Hi," he said, as if he hadn't already greeted her.

"Um, hi," she said. "Aiden, this is my friend Frank"—she fingerspelled the name. "Frank, this is my son Aiden."

"Hi," Frank said again. He fingerspelled h-i, doing a creditable job.

Aiden spelled h-i back, a little wide-eyed.

"I hear you like hot dogs," Frank said, making the sign for hot dog. "Me too."

Aiden looked at Teresa and back at him. "S-W-A-T?"

"SWAT," she interpreted for Frank. "Yes."

The boy's eyes grew wider. "You shoot bad men?" he signed, and Teresa translated.

"If I have to."

"Can I see your gun?"

"He wants to see your gun," she said faintly. She hated the very idea.

"I don't have it with me," he said. He made eye contact with Aiden and didn't raise his voice. He waited for her to interpret and then said, "Another time."

"Cool," Aiden said, barely audible but using his voice. She gave Frank a look: *Leave 'em wanting more.*

"I have to go," he said. "It was nice to meet you, Aiden. Maybe I'll see you both at Oktoberfest." She watched him go before she turned her attention back to her son. He looked absolutely thrilled. Clearly, accepting Frank was not going to be a problem. How close he would want to get was another matter.

****

She called Frank when Aiden was asleep. "You blindsided me," she complained.

"I thought it would be better if it was more spontaneous," he said. "I love it when you call me, even if it's to tell me off." His voice was so warm and intimate in her ear, making her feel very close to him. "I think the meeting went pretty well, don't you?"

"Yes, he was very impressed."

"Where would you like to meet on Saturday?" he asked.

"You don't want to be spontaneous?"

"I don't want to wander around hunting for you."

He demonstrated plaintively: "Teresa! Teresa! Where are you?"

She laughed. "Dope!"

"I love your laugh," he said. "I'd like to come over right now. Is Aiden in bed?"

"Yes. And no, it's not going to happen."

"I know, I know: be patient. This thing starts at nine? Is parking a problem?"

"It's free on the streets if you're early enough, or there are lots where you can park for a few dollars, and the money goes to charities."

"How about if I sit in the parking lot and watch for you and just happen to come up behind you?"

"A little obvious," she said, laughing. "They're supposed to have a dachshund race—Aiden will want to see the puppies, so we'll go there first."

"A boy needs a dog," he said.

"I have all I can do to take care of Aiden and myself."

"So you wouldn't want me to give him one?"

"No. Why? Do you have a spare one around somewhere? I think you've given us too much already."

He sighed. "Slow and steady wins the race," he said.

"Well, it works for the dachshunds."

Chapter 12

The dachshunds weren't slow or steady, but they were very cute. Eight dogs were entered, a lot for so small a venue. Four were only puppies, and they were all amateurs—a good thing, as constant racing would have been abusive. Most of them didn't run at all. The boldest three dashed across the course to their waiting masters, and it was nearly a photo finish. None of the spectators cared, least of all Aiden, who squatted to pet the most sociable pair.

"Hi," Frank said behind Teresa.

She hadn't been thinking about him, totally focused on her son and the dogs, but she was very glad to see him. He looked great, tan and rested. He gave her a quick squeeze while Aiden wasn't looking, and they walked together to join him. At the last second, he took her hand, and she couldn't pull away without being obvious. She didn't think it was a good idea, but she liked the way it felt.

If the boy noticed, he gave no sign. He looked up at Frank, plainly awed. Frank signed, "Hello."

"Hi," Aiden said shyly. Curiosity won out over diffidence, and he signed, "Have your gun?" Teresa translated.

"Not today. I'm not working today. I'm here to have fun." She slipped her hand out of his to translate. She couldn't tell if Aiden was disappointed. "Where shall we go next?" Frank asked.

Aiden took a second to understand he was the one being asked. He shrugged, looked at his mother, and then signed, "Dance?"

"Folk dancing," she explained. "He likes to watch."

"He can't hear the music…?"

"He can feel the vibrations underfoot, and he likes the costumes and the movement—it really is something to watch. Pretty girls—you should enjoy that."

"I only have eyes for you," he said. Aiden couldn't follow the conversation, and she didn't try to interpret. Frank took her hand, and the three of them strolled slowly toward the music stage, pausing to look at toys and handicrafts in the booths. Aiden seemed to have taken it for granted that Frank was part of their group. Maybe he simply missed having a man around—if it couldn't be Brett, Frank would do as a substitute.

They stood next to the bleachers, and Aiden scrambled ahead, perched on a seat a few rows closer, and watched intently, swinging his legs. In spite of his denial, Teresa could tell Frank liked watching as the young girls twirled and lifted their skirts. It was a very pretty, lively dance, with quick steps and intricate maneuvers. When it was over, they applauded enthusiastically, and she glanced around at the dozens of people who had gathered to watch. It was then that she noticed Brett.

He had seen Aiden and started toward him and then stopped, hesitating. The boy was still watching the stage, his back to them. Brett approached him, and he stood up, both eager and wary. Brett signed something she didn't catch, and Aiden pointed toward her. Brett ran his eyes along the rows of bleachers and found her just as Frank turned to see what she was looking at. He took a step forward.

Brett had seen him too, now, and he walked toward them, his fists clenching and unclenching. She knew him well enough to know it was probably just nerves, but he looked hostile. "Teresa," he said hoarsely, a little out of breath. He stopped, uncertain, and then managed to say politely, "Hi. How are you?"

Frank stepped in front of her. "What's it to you?" he asked. "How's Lacey?"

Brett turned red. "Christ!" he said. "I don't give a damn about Lacey." He said the name with something like contempt.

Frank started to speak, and Teresa put an urgent hand on his arm. They were both intelligent, rational men, and she was astonished by this immediate, fierce antagonism between them. She supposed it was sheer sexual jealousy, which she ought to understand, but her own bitterness paled before this testosterone-fueled rage.

She did not want them to fight, especially not in front of Aiden, who was momentarily distracted by a little girl curtsying on stage. "Let me talk to him for a minute," she said and gestured to Brett to walk away toward a leather-crafts booth. "Stay with Aiden," she told Frank firmly.

She wasn't sure what she intended to say, but Brett spoke first, angry and out of breath. "Alix told me you went away for the weekend with this guy. You had sex with him?" He was outraged.

"Keep your voice down," she said coldly. "It's none of your business."

"Were you trying to get even?"

"No, I wasn't trying to get even. I didn't get even. I'm moving on, and so should you."

"I *can't*," he said. He had tears in his eyes—anger, futility, loss?—and it hurt to see him suffering so much. No matter what he had done, she didn't like hurting him. They had been too close for too long. "I love you," he said. "I need you to forgive me. And this guy—I don't like him. He's not right for you."

"You don't even know him."

"What do you see in him? What does he have? Money? Is it money? He makes a lot?"

"If that's all you think of me—"

"What, then? I didn't think you went for his type."

"He's not a type. He's a nice guy who treats me right. He can hold his liquor, and he doesn't cheat."

"I don't cheat!" Brett said furiously. "That's not who I am, and you know it. It was one time, one damn time, one stupid mistake I'll regret for the rest of my life! I got fired, and I got drunk, and Lacey was *there,* and I guess I was—"

"What?"

"Looking for…I don't know…comfort." He knew it was a weak excuse and couldn't meet her eyes. He looked away toward the bleachers, where music was now playing

"You couldn't get it from me?"

"I was drunk. I…I wanted it to be more than that with you."

"Well, you didn't make it more. You made it less."

"I don't know what else I can say except I'm sorry. If you give me another chance, I promise I'll do whatever I can to work things out. We can go to couples therapy, and I'll...I don't know, talk to you about the hard stuff...I haven't had a drink since that night. I'll go to AA if you want."

"I don't want anything except to be left alone. It's finished. Get over it." She walked away and didn't look back. The dancing had started again, the wonderful weaver's dance she remembered from the previous year. Frank was standing where they had been before, watching intently. She couldn't see Aiden in front of him, and when he moved and she had a clear view of the seats beyond him, she still didn't see Aiden.

Her heart beat a little faster, but she made herself stay calm and not overreact. She glanced around and touched Frank's arm. "Where's Aiden?"

He looked automatically where she had and then around them. "He was right here, Teresa, I swear. I saw him a second ago." He was anxious now and took her hand and squeezed it tightly, but in the next second he shifted into macho mode, calm and purposeful. He released her hand. "He can't have gone far. We'll find him." He glanced around again and called, "Aiden!"

"He can't hear you," she reminded him gently. She tried to think rationally, but she was scared shitless—every mother's nightmare, a lost child. Losing track of him, even for seconds, was the worst thing she could face. In mere seconds children had disappeared forever. She went quickly toward the stage and looked back, taking in the whole crowd. She turned all the way around, searching hard. Frank was looking too. It would have made more sense for them to separate, but he stayed close to her. She took a deep breath. "There's a public address system," she said. "We can ask people if they see him." She couldn't remember where the Lost and Found was—in one of the buildings near the entrance?

And then she saw him. He had his back to them, but she couldn't miss him anywhere. He was hers, a precious little life she valued more than her own. He was only yards from the stage, watching a man demonstrate a silly clown toy. Trying not to cry with relief, Teresa walked up and hugged him from behind. He didn't even look around. He knew it was her and leaned back against her.

She looked at Frank. His face was a study—relief, guilt, probably residual anger at Brett. "I'm so sorry," he said. "I barely took my eyes off him. The very first time you trusted me with your son!"

She let go of Aiden to pat his arm. "It happens."

They were both a little shaky from the fright and relief, but Aiden was completely oblivious. He pointed at the clown. "Can I have?" he signed.

"What?" she asked, deliberately dense.

He didn't know the sign or couldn't think of it. "Clown," he said, doing very well with the difficult diphthong.

Teresa hugged him. She glanced at the price on the hanging toys and nodded. She opened her purse, but Frank stepped in to pay for it.

After that little scare, the rest of the day was pretty lighthearted. They strolled, browsed in booths, and watched more dancing and strolling musicians in costume. Aiden wasn't quite old enough to disdain the kiddie rides, and Frank kept paying for him to ride until he was dizzy.

In such a small town, it was inevitable they would encounter people Teresa knew. She introduced Frank, without a qualifier, saying simply, "Frank McAllister," and sometimes, "He's new in town." She was a little self-conscious when she saw people make note of their linked hands and probably wonder what a hot guy like him was doing with her. If they knew Brett, she was also afraid they wouldn't know what he had done and would think she had dumped him for Frank, or if they did know would judge her indecent haste in moving on.

Delicious smells wafted toward them from every direction, and when the sun was overhead they sat on wooden benches to eat. Frank told Aiden bratwurst was a German hot dog, and he ate it happily with mustard and sauerkraut. "You don't let him eat hot dogs every day, do you?" Frank asked.

"Once a week, usually. Today is extra." She bit into her hot meat and cabbage pie to keep from adding something more defensive. She didn't much like bachelor Frank questioning her parenting skills, but she supposed he meant it as friendly concern. Aiden was more and more comfortable with him and grilled him about police work in ways that challenged her interpreting skills. She had to spell most of the terminology. She learned a lot too—his job was far more complex and wide-ranging than she had supposed.

When he told them the story about the drunk who had hit him with a bottle, Aiden admonished him, signing, "Always wear your hard hat." Teresa translated, using "helmet" for hard hat and finger-spelled the word for Aiden, who gamely sounded out, "Hel-met." His willingness to use his voice in public was increasing by leaps and bounds. She reflected that the moments when he was missing had made Frank more patient and indulgent with him than he might

115

otherwise have been. He also seemed to have forgotten about the confrontation with Brett. On Aiden's side, hero worship worked wonders. He even let Frank take him to the men's room, probably happy not to be treated like a mama's boy.

When they had seen everything they wanted to see, they agreed to call it a day and started toward the parking lot. "Want to do something tomorrow?" Frank asked. Instead of translating, she shook her head slightly, and he asked, "Next week?"

She silently assented. "Aiden? Shall we do something with Frank next week?"

"What?" he asked eagerly. She supposed he hoped for something like a SWAT operation.

Frank touched his arm and fingerspelled z-o-o. "Do you like the zoo?"

"Yes!" Powell City had a very fine zoo, and he had only been once.

"You learned the manual alphabet?" she asked, surprised and touched.

"I'm trying," he said. "I'm afraid that's all I have today." As they crossed the street to the parking lot, he commented, "And a good time was had by all."

He was holding her hand, and she gave his an answering squeeze. "Yes, it went well," she agreed.

They stopped beside the pickup, and Aiden leaned against Teresa. "Is this thing safe?" Frank asked. "You should have—"

"Don't even start," she said.

"Aren't children supposed to sit in the back seat?"

"As if I had one. I don't have airbags either. Nobody in Cougar enforces those rules anyway. I drive carefully, and we always buckle up."

She got Aiden's attention. "We buckle up, right?"

He nodded. He was drooping a little, perhaps tired from all the excitement.

"Take care of your mother," Frank told him. Aiden squinted up at him, trying to read his lips. When Teresa translated, he stood a little taller and took her hand protectively. Frank backed away, smiling, toward his SUV.

"Bye," Aiden called.

"Bye, Champ."

Teresa translated it as "champion." She didn't know how to explain in sign language and said aloud, "A nickname."

On the way home in the pickup, Aiden leaned against the door. He knew she wasn't supposed to take her eyes off the road, so he used his voice to comment on the festival. He had the clown toy in a bag clutched tight in his lap. He waited until they got home to say, "I miss Brett."

"I know, sweetie. So do I." Did she? She kissed his forehead and asked, "Do you like Frank?"

He thought about it, and then he nodded. Before she could take a breath of relief, he signed emphatically, "He not Brett," and, making an effort, said aloud, "He not—"

"He's," she corrected. Those pesky *be* verbs!

"He's not Brett."

"No, I know. But you can be friends with them both." *Over their dead bodies!* "You can be friends with Brett even if we don't see him anymore." He frowned, puzzled. "You can still like him," she said.

"You still like him?"

Put on the spot, Teresa groped for a wise answer,

but the best she could do was, "I don't know." She supposed she would eventually get past the hurt enough to remember they had been friends for a long time before they became a couple, and maybe they could be friends again. Maybe when he was past it too and accepted her relationship with Frank. She now had to take it for granted that she would have one.

****

She gave up the idea of returning the cell phones to Frank. What would he do with them? Drive back to the coast to return them? It would be a pointless gesture and invite a charge of ingratitude. She was more comfortable with using hers, although she would never use all its features, and now she tackled Aiden's.

She studied the small print of the instruction book and consulted her well-thumbed sign-language dictionary, but in the end, it was all a waste of time. Aiden proudly showed it to Sasha, and in five minutes she had him texting like a pro. "Golly shakes!" she said. "Some phone!"

"Well, you were right," Teresa told Frank during what had now become a nightly call. "He and Sasha text each other all the time now, and it *is* helping his reading, if not his grammar and spelling. As long as some big kid doesn't beat him up and take it…"

"Want me to teach him self-defense?"

"He's a child!"

"He's old enough to learn to block a punch."

"Just don't teach him to hit first." She sighed. "Sasha teaches him to text. You teach him to defend himself. I'm starting to feel inadequate."

"But that's the way it's supposed to be. It takes a village. You do all the hard stuff, the daily grind, so you deserve whatever help the rest of us can give you."

****

Frank joined Teresa and Aiden at the grill on Thursday night. He was drinking beer at the bar and watching the World Series game when they arrived. He ordered hot dogs and macaroni and cheese in solidarity with Aiden, and they compared notes—Frank liked catsup on his hot dog and Aiden mustard, Frank preferred whole wheat buns, Aiden liked his macaroni and cheese a little soupy, and so on. When the conversation moved on to more adult matters, the children started texting each other and giggling. "Is it a good idea to have your six-year-old hang out in a bar so much?" Frank asked.

"It's a family restaurant that serves beer, not a bar. We've been doing this Thursday night thing for years, and we would both miss it."

"It's a tradition. I get that. But you can always make new ones." He always said things like that so blithely, as if he couldn't imagine they would make her uneasy. They did, but everything else counterbalanced the feeling. He was great with Aiden, especially considering his lack of experience with children. He was great with her too, except for making her feel a little crowded at times.

When they finished eating, he was watching the game again and didn't try to kiss her in front of Aiden. "I'll see you both Saturday," he promised.

Chapter 13

The zoo was even more of a success than Oktoberfest, especially from Aiden's point of view. He was fascinated by all the animals and could have happily spent all day in front of the tiger enclosure if there hadn't been so much more to see. He had so much energy, running back and forth while Frank and Teresa walked slowly, hand in hand. She felt more comfortable about public displays here, freer, knowing they were unlikely to run into anybody they knew.

"Does he ever run down?" Frank asked, amused, as Aiden raced back to them for the umpteenth time.

"Not before dinnertime. Sometimes I wish he could give me an energy transfusion."

The boy was so constantly entertained that all they needed to do was keep an eye out to be sure he didn't disappear in the crowd and try to answer his millions of questions: Why do giraffes have such long necks? How high can a kangaroo jump? Does a warthog have warts? He also undertook to teach Frank some of the appropriate sign language—monkey, lion, peacock, elephant, duck, snake, and so on. "I'll never remember them all," Frank said. "I don't know how you do it."

Teresa jumped when an elephant trumpeted loudly right next to them. Aiden was facing in the other direction and didn't react at all. Frank said, "There's another reason why the cochlear implant should be done as soon as possible. Even if it's only partially successful, he should be able to hear what's coming—a car honking, somebody yelling. Just to keep him safe, I'd think you'd want to—"

"Of course I do," she said.

"We're agreed, then. As soon as we're married, I'll have you both put on my insurance, and we can do it right away."

"Frank!"

"What? Oh, sorry, I know I have to do it formally. I've been looking at rings."

"You have?" The possibility hadn't occurred to her at all. She had never had one—Gene hadn't been able to afford it when they married so young.

"Yes," he said, maybe a bit sheepish. "Would you prefer to choose one together? I know a lot of women like to have a say, but I kind of wanted to surprise you."

"I don't know. I hadn't thought about it. It seems like it's a little soon," she suggested tentatively.

"If we're sure, why wait?"

"But are we?"

"I am. I knew right away. Can you explain to me why you're holding back? You have doubts about me?"

"I can't figure out why a great guy like you is interested in me."

"You're kidding, right? You can't possibly have self-esteem issues."

She shrugged. "I guess it's just general caution. It's almost too good to be true. And most people know each other longer first, especially these days. I've been burned once. I don't want another divorce."

"No, of course not. How can I reassure you?"

"Just...slow down a little. Alix mentioned the other

day that wanting to rush into a relationship is one of the warning signs of abuse, and I know you wouldn't want me to think—"

"Teresa," he said reproachfully. "You are sacred to me. I would never harm a hair on your head."

"Sacred? Really, Frank, it's embarrassing when you lay it on so thick."

He kissed her temple penitently. "I know. I'm sorry. I can't seem to help myself. I've never felt anything quite like this."

"Not with…your wife?"

"No, that was a little different. I mean it was good; we had a great relationship, but I think you're the one I was meant to be with. I wish you were as sure as I am. It's a great feeling. We can get married and buy a house together—in Cougar, of course; I assume you don't want to live in Powell City—and we'll have a little girl right away, and you can stay home and take care of them and study for your degree."

"Do I get a say in any of this?"

"Yes, of course, but I'm sure we want the same things. I'd like more kids, but if you don't, I'll settle for two, and eventually you can open your own practice or at least be a full partner where you are."

"That does sound good," she admitted.

"Your parents live here in the city, right? When can I meet them?" Teresa was torn. She both wanted to introduce Frank to her family and dreaded the upheaval it would cause. He noticed her reluctance and asked, "You're afraid your folks won't like me? Do they have something against cops or…?"

"No, but they'll think it's too fast."

"When they see us together, they'll understand."

She wasn't so sure, but what could she say? "Would you be able to get off work at Thanksgiving?"

"I'll see what I can do, but let's not wait that long. We could take them out to dinner—we'll choose a casual family restaurant. Aiden too, of course. I should ask your dad for permission to propose to you."

"That's a pretty old-fashioned idea." She could imagine exactly how it would play out.

"What does he do, your father?"

"He works for a company called Information Management. It sounds important, but he says he's a glorified typist. It's a lot different from farming. He—actually, both of them—will think it's too soon—after Brett."

Aiden ran back to them, signing excitedly, "Come see rhinoceros!" He grabbed Teresa's hand and swung it as they walked. "Rhino...sir?"

"Rhine-oss-erus," she enunciated.

"Rhinoceros!" He liked the word.

"Very good." He ran ahead and ran his finger along the sign in front of the enclosure, puzzling out the words.

"He's pretty verbal, considering, isn't he?" Frank asked. "I'm not sure what's normal at his age."

"They say children who learn a second language at an early age find it easier to learn everything else."

"A second—oh, you mean sign language?"

"ASL, yes. And he learned the manual alphabet and the printed alphabet at the same time too."

"I know how challenging that is," he said. They dutifully admired the rhinoceros, and then Frank asked, "What were we talking about before?" Teresa was going to say something about their future plans or her parents, but he said, "Oh, yes, Devlin. I found out why he was fired."

"I didn't want you to do that." Hadn't she in fact asked him not to? "I wanted *him* to tell me, and he wouldn't, but now it's not my business." She had wanted to know, and she had wanted Brett to be able to tell her anything. She was also afraid to know. He wouldn't have been fired for sleeping with Lacey, so it had to be something worse—worse than the calamity that toppled the life they had planned to have together.

"Good," Frank said. "That means you're moving on. Still…didn't you even want to know if it was something that could have put your son at risk?"

"Was it?"

"No, but it might have involved Aiden." He came to a full stop, but of course now she had to know. She gave him a look, and he smiled and touched her hair affectionately. "He falsified information on a grant application."

"Really?" It didn't sound like Brett, but neither did cheating with a teenage waitress. She had always believed he was honest—he couldn't even lie about Lacey. "What does it have to do with Aiden?"

"My understanding is the school district has to pay for a sign-language interpreter under the ADA, but other things—like the after-school program and the speech therapist—were paid for by this grant. Devlin falsified information—I'm not sure what. Maybe inflated the number of disabled students, something like that. And of course Aiden was the beneficiary, so it's a conflict of interest, because you were dating."

This was a double blow. "So we'll lose the therapist?"

"Don't worry about it. You'll be home when he gets out of school, and we can afford a private therapist."

"If we get married."

"Well...of course it's up to you. I can understand why you wouldn't want to be a cop's wife."

She hadn't really considered it much, but now she remembered what it was like to try to sleep while he was involved in a six-hour standoff before they'd even had a first date. "Was it hard on her?" she asked, and tentatively, "Your first wife?"

He liked that. He put his arm around her and held her close. "Nikki was a pro," he said.

"Nikki?" She felt both guilt for the information she had gained secretly, and a leap of surprised hope. Maybe he hadn't been married to the mysterious Edris after all.

"Yeah, that was her name, or what everybody called her, anyway. Her middle name was Nicole. Anyway, her father and brother were both cops, and she worked for the department as a computer tech, so she didn't go into it blind. If that's one of the things standing in your way, maybe it would help if I showed you all the precautions we take, the safety equipment and so on."

Aiden tugged at Teresa's hand, and she followed him and helped him read a sign. When he was satisfied, he signed, "What you and Frank talk about?" The sign they had devised for his name combined F with the sign for police. Frank was right behind them now, and she interpreted the question for him.

"Police work," he said.

Aiden, hanging on the fence of the enclosure,

looked up at him. "When can I see your gun?"

Frank glanced at Teresa. "I don't think your mom wants you to."

"Why not?"

"Guns are dangerous," she told him. "They scare me."

"Yes, they're dangerous," Frank agreed. "That's why it's very important to learn the right way to use them. When you're a little older, I'll take you to the shooting range and teach you how to do it safely." She cringed, but translated it all.

"How much old?" Aiden signed.

Frank deferred to Teresa. "Thirty," she said.

He shook his head, amused. "Eight? Twelve?"

"Twenty-one."

"Okay," he said. "We'll leave it for a later negotiation. I'll show you first, so you'll know how careful we would be. I will bring the gun—unloaded—for him to see one day soon."

She didn't like the idea, but it wasn't unreasonable. She relayed the promise to Aiden.

The weather was still pleasant, so they ate lunch on a tree-lined deck. Teresa expected Aiden to insist on a hot dog, but when Frank opted for a grilled chicken sandwich, he wanted one too. It came with a slice of cheese, which he liked, and lettuce and tomato to satisfy her. She wanted him to have milk, but Frank chose Coke, so she let Aiden have one—"just this once." He watched Frank eat and copied him, bite for bite, sip for sip.

She couldn't help laughing. "You little monkey!" she said. Even if they didn't get married, this was so good for Aiden, in a way even Brett hadn't been.

Frank hadn't noticed what was happening and grinned when he caught on. He met Aiden's eyes and asked, "Are you having fun?" Aiden looked at her for the translation and nodded vigorously. "What's your favorite animal so far?"

He gave the question serious thought. "Tiger baby," he signed.

"Tiger cub," she said, and spelled C-U-B for Aiden.

"What your favorite?" he asked Frank very clearly. He glanced at his mother and amended it: "What *is* your favorite?" She had tears in her eyes she didn't want either of them to see. A whole sentence, in a crowded public place, where she had seen curious stares for the signing!

"Hmm…" Frank considered. "The rhinoceros," he said finally. "I like its name."

Aiden frowned, concentrating hard and absentmindedly kicking the table leg. He held up one finger. "Tiger." He held up two. "Rhine-oss-ur-us!" Frank put up his hand, and they high-fived each other.

"Okay, what's *your* favorite?" Frank asked Teresa. He managed a good approximation of the sign for favorite.

"I'm not sure. Meerkats, maybe."

"What's next?" Frank asked Aiden. "What do you like that we haven't seen yet?"

He kicked the table leg. "Polar bear," he signed and after a moment's consideration, "Tiger again."

****

On the way home, with Aiden in the back seat texting to Sasha, Frank said, "I have to work next weekend, but the week after, if the weather isn't bad, we could drive to the coast and take Aiden with us. He could sleep in the loft." She didn't answer, and he gave her a quick glance. "I keep thinking about how wonderful it was in the hotel, with the sound of the surf, sleeping with you in my arms all night."

"I don't think so," she said. "Maybe just to Genoa to the aquarium and back the same day. We could go even if it rains."

"In that case, maybe we could take in a movie on Sunday. An animated Disney picture is playing at the theater here, and it's supposed to be good. Might be time to try Aiden on the captions again?"

"It would be worth a try," Teresa said. "Even if he couldn't understand everything, he would probably enjoy the movie. It would have to be in the afternoon, after church."

"Agreed, but it's two weeks away. I could die of neglect in two weeks." He glanced in the rearview mirror. "When can we make love again?"

Teresa punched his arm playfully. "Is that all you ever think about?"

"I think I've been very patient."

"Yes, you have."

"I'm sort of assuming I'm not the only one who wants this. Please tell me if I'm wrong. We could do lunch again. Skip the Spicy Burger—I'll get takeout and pick you up. Or you have Monday mornings off, right? I could swing that when I work the weekend."

"I usually do laundry and things like that, and sometimes Alix comes over for coffee."

"Tell her you're busy. You can skip the girl talk for once, and I'll help you with the laundry."

"Help me get the sheets dirty, you mean?"

Chapter 14

"You know," Alix said, when Teresa recounted the conversation at the zoo over coffee in her kitchen on Monday morning, "this is starting to sound familiar. The rushing, the exaggerated compliments, the rosy picture of the future. It's possible Frank might be mentally ill."

"Oh, of course!" Teresa said, slapping her forehead. "How could I have missed that? He has to be crazy to find me attractive."

"You *are* attractive, Terror," Alix said warmly. "I'd totally do you if I was a lesbian—which would be kind of cool, you know; no masculine ego to tend. Here's what else is attractive about you: If he wants children, you're already a mother, so he knows you're fertile and good with kids. You have no close family in town to interfere with the relationship. You need everything he has to offer, so you'll be grateful and let him have his way. Damn fine wife material!"

"So you think he likes me because I'm needy?"

"You need financial help, emotional support, a father figure for your son, not to mention the cochlear implant he could pay for, decent sex, somebody who's good at fixing things, protection from the big bad world…"

"Gee, Alix, are you trying to convince me to marry him or slit my wrists? Golly shakes, as Sasha would say!"

"She does have a way with words. But seriously, he doesn't just find you attractive; he thinks you're the goddamned love of his life. I'm not saying he's certifiable, but I used to work with a cook when I was waitressing who would have these grandiose plans for buying real estate and spend a lot of money on antique furniture and be on the phone for hours doing fabulous deals, and then he would crash and be depressed and stare at the walls. He got fired, of course, but I heard he was doing fine after he got on the right meds. Frank might be in the manic stage of bipolar disorder—high functioning, if his job hasn't been affected, and I'm sure the police department keeps a close eye on those things. They probably do random drug tests and wouldn't have hired him if he was on medication. He might not need medication. He might be fine without it, just a little exuberant—but don't get too committed until you've seen the other end of the spectrum."

Teresa sipped her coffee and waited. She didn't know what she was waiting for. An argument to counter with? For Alix to say she was joking or take it back? A sense of clarity on the whole question? What if she was right? What would be best to do? She had been pretty honest with Frank about her feelings—he had asked for no bullshit. Should she present him with this theory and see what he would say? Or run like hell for her safety and Aiden's?

"Say something," Alix prompted.

"You're practicing psychiatry without a license," she said.

"Yup," Alix agreed. "You got me. So…besides the predictions of wedded bliss, did you have fun?"

"Yes," Teresa said emphatically, not without a sigh of relief. "It was *so* good for Aiden, and I didn't think it was possible this soon after Brett."

"Yeah, Frank *is* a charmer. I'll give you that."

****

His charm was very much in evidence on Thursday when he picked her up at the Rosey Lane Veterinary Clinic at lunchtime. He was in a very good mood and obviously pleased to see her, kissing her lovingly before he started the car. "You look great," he said and kissed her again. He was in uniform, or half in uniform—black trousers and long-sleeved shirt with PCPD above the pocket and a SWAT patch on the sleeve. She was wearing the sea anemone T-shirt, which she hadn't worn since the Sunday at the coast. It wasn't exactly her style, but it was flattering, and he would know she had worn it for him. He had the radio on—Willie Nelson singing "You Were Always on My Mind." Something smelled good—Chinese takeout containers on the back seat. He caught her looking and said, "Chinese chicken salad. I didn't think you'd want anything with onions or chili peppers."

"Perfect," she said.

They had talked on the phone the night before, but he asked, "How are you? Everything okay?" He was edgy in an excited, upbeat way. She couldn't help remembering Alix's bipolar diagnosis, but maybe it had more to do with the fact that they hadn't had sex in two weeks and were presumably about to.

They ate lunch first, sitting at his kitchen table, not rushing, but not wasting time, since she needed to get back to work. The salad was delicious, with crispy noodles and sweet, spicy sesame sauce. They talked easily, very comfortable with each other now, and Frank had trouble keeping his hands off her. He touched her hand, brushed her hair back from her face, let his fingers drift toward the deep V of her neckline. "So, Halloween tonight," he said. "Will you still be at the grill for dinner?"

"Yes, we'll go trick-or-treating after. Two guesses what Aiden's costume is."

"Tiger? No? Zookeeper!"

"No, Frank. Think about it. He's going as a police officer."

His hand went to his heart. "No shit? Would he like to borrow a badge? Nothing else would fit him, I'm afraid."

"Oh, Frank, he would love that!"

"Don't let me forget to give it to you when we leave."

When they got to the fortune cookies, they proved to be chocolate-covered, something she had never seen before. "They're from this little place where they make them to order," he explained. "Any flavor you want."

He handed her one, and she automatically split it. She had seen some pretty bizarre fortunes and was ready to laugh and shake her head, but this one said *Will you marry me?* Apparently the fortunes could be made to order too.

She hadn't seen it coming, and she should have. She was stunned into immobility, and when she looked up, he was smiling, eager. "I love you, Teresa." He touched her face and leaned in for a kiss. "You have such a beautiful name," he said. "I think Teresa McAllister has a nice *ring*," and he held the ring up, offering it to her.

She took it slowly, numbly. It was exquisite, a tapered channel-set diamond band with a cushion-cut center diamond. His tendency to exaggerate every compliment might have led her to expect this to be overdone too, but it was not far off what she might have chosen herself if she could have: clearly expensive but not gaudy, the diamond not so large it would overwhelm her slender finger. When he was sure she'd had a good look, he took her hand and slipped it on. Teresa was not immune to the drama of the occasion—she tilted her hand so the gems would catch the light. "It's beautiful," she breathed.

She expected him to press her for an answer, but he took her into the bedroom instead. Teresa sat on the bed and started to take off her shirt—they had no time to waste—but Frank said, "Let me." He pulled it off over her head and kissed her. She reached behind her back, but he said, "Leave your bra on."

"Why?"

"I don't know; I just like it that way." She remembered she had worn a halter top the first time, and hadn't removed her bra last time, either. As a quirk, she much preferred it to handcuffs. It wasn't as if he didn't like her breasts—his fingers were inside the bra, and he kissed her intensely, easing her back against the pillows to kiss her everywhere.

He took off her shoes, and she lifted her hips so he could pull off her jeans. "I love making love to you," he said. "There's something mysterious, almost aloof about you, but your body is so responsive, so sweet all over. Your mouth, your breasts…"

As good as it had been before, this time was that much better. He made such tender, passionate love to her that she cried out, "Oh, God, Frank! I love you!"—not even realizing it was the first time she had said the words. If her body was responsive, his was very much in charge, and with something like triumph he took her wrists and held them above her head as he brought her to an intense simultaneous climax.

Lying in his arms, waiting for her breathing to slow, she felt so good—safe, blissful, very loving, very loved. She ran a hand over his chest, liking the feel of his warm skin, filled with tenderness toward him. If she married him, they would no longer have to disrupt their days to grab a few minutes together. Alix was right; she should know him longer, but engagements could be long, could be broken if necessary. She would have time to be sure before she was committed forever, and it was always possible everything would be all right and she would be happy. "Yes," she said. "I will marry you." It wasn't hard. Making it easy to say yes was what he did best.

He kissed the top of her head. "After we're married, there won't be anything to keep us from sleeping in the same bed every night."

"Unless you're out getting shot at."

"I'll always come home to you, though."

She drifted a little, savoring the promise, and then she remembered—"I have to get back to work."

"Call in sick."

"I can't. Veronica's counting on me. What time is it?" She consulted her watch. "Oh!" She got out of bed, found her clothes, and rushed into the bathroom to wash up. She studied herself in the mirror—God! Veronica would know right away. She splashed water on her face, combed her hair, put on fresh lipstick, and, unable to resist the temptation, opened the medicine cabinet.

If he was bipolar, there was no medication for it here. He wasn't taking uppers, either. There were no stimulants of any kind and no sleep aids—he must have a clear conscience and a cast-iron stomach. Plain aspirin and eye drops were as far as he went.

When she came out, he was still lying lazily against the pillows. "Get dressed, Frank. You have to drive me back."

"There's the practical, hard-headed Teresa we all know and love," he said. He dressed quickly and then took her in his arms and kissed her. "I love you," he said.

"Are you always like this?" she asked, disentangling herself to retrieve her shoes. "Don't you ever get down or depressed?"

"It would be a waste of time," he said dismissively. "I guess it was pretty depressing when I thought you were married to Devlin, but there's no percentage in getting discouraged. You have to push through the hard stuff and do whatever is necessary."

"You do know most people aren't as strong-minded as you? It's what makes you a good cop, I guess."

He gave her the bag of chocolate fortune cookies and remembered to find a badge for Aiden. It was not his current one, which he would need, but one from the Genoa PD. "I won't be able to stop by the grill tonight," he said, "so be sure to take pictures of him in his costume."

In the car he asked, "What kind of wedding do you want? If you've always wanted a big, fancy wedding, we can do that, or a small, quiet ceremony in the church here, whatever you want."

"I guess I'll have to think about it."

"Traditional vows or one of these modern make-up-your-own ceremonies?"

"Traditional all the way."

He was pleased. "Yeah? Will you promise to obey, or are you too women's lib?"

"If I did, I might have to break it."

"I can't wait to see you in a wedding dress, all in white, a veil over your beautiful hair—or barefoot on the beach with flowers in your hair, if that's what you want." Teresa stared out the window and didn't say anything. "What are you thinking?" he asked. "No bullshit now."

"My parents," she said.

"I meant to ask your dad first, but I couldn't wait."

Teresa smiled to think how astonished her father would have been by such a question. "They're not *that* old-fashioned," she said, "but they are traditional enough not to approve of a big wedding or a white dress for a second marriage. They might not even come—my father gave me away once, and they expected me to stay put."

"They sound pretty unforgiving."

"They wouldn't see it that way. Would any of your family come?"

He considered. "My sister Kathleen will want to be there. Otherwise, it's a long way to travel."

"Richard would come," she said, with something like relief. "He might be willing to walk me down the aisle."

"One sibling each," he said, "a minister, and you and me; what more do we need?"

"Alix, of course," she said, "and Aiden and Sasha. You should have a best man."

"I can handle that," he said, but something grim had crept into his voice. He didn't like Alix's language or Sasha's manners? But they did know how to behave in church!

****

When they entered the Cougar Bar & Grill, the Halloween decorations that had been up for most of October had been supplemented by jack-o'-lanterns with flickering lights inside and black-and-orange napkins at each table setting. Teresa had traded her sea anemone shirt for a more comfortable one that read *This IS My Halloween Costume.* Aiden wore black jeans and T-shirt, and Teresa had cut the sleeves off an outgrown windbreaker to make a vest, with duct tape letters spelling SWAT on the back. His helmet was cheap plastic from the dollar store, but the badge pinned to the front of his vest was the genuine article. He swaggered a bit, his usual shyness swallowed up in this exciting new identity.

"The SWAT team's here!" Alix shouted. Sasha, in a long skirt and pointed black hat, was a witch with a big green wart on her nose. She gave Aiden a grin of approval and twirled to show off her own getup. Hand in hand, they headed back to the corner booth. "Hey, Terror," Alix said, swiping at the bar with a damp rag. "Have you seen McDreamy today? Get it? McAllister…"

"Uh, yeah. We had lunch."

Alix leered. "Did you have a nice *lunch*?"

"Yes," she said demurely. "Chinese." She leaned in to be heard above the buzz of voices without raising her own. "Did you ever do it with your bra on?"

"Sure. When I lost my virginity in the back seat of Mike Halliday's jalopy. He couldn't get the damn thing unhooked." Maybe that was all it was with Frank, Teresa thought: a flashback to high school, a taste of forbidden fruit—and to her a reminder of the fabulous Grey Harbor massage.

Very casually, she lifted her left hand and pretended to stifle a yawn.

"Oh, my God!" Alix cried. "He didn't! That is so great! Let me see." She held Teresa's hand tight in hers, turning it to make the diamonds sparkle. "It's gotta be a couple thousand dollars at least!"

"Do you think so?"

"Three, four thousand, maybe." Alix was ecstatic, but Teresa couldn't help wondering if she was worth such an investment. "Does Aiden know?"

"No, bless his heart; he probably thinks it's part of my costume. Halloween is enough excitement for tonight."

****

When they had eaten dinner, enhanced by pumpkin cookies fresh from the oven, they headed out trick-or-treating. Little witch Sasha was part of their party too, since her mother had her hands full at the grill. The night was cold and clear, with only a crescent moon. Teresa carried a flashlight to guide them from one street light or porch light to the next. Last year, Aiden had still been very shy, overwhelmed by excited attention he couldn't understand, but now he had more savoir faire, knowing none of it was important, and very proud of his costume.

She let each of the children choose two pieces of

candy to eat right away, returned Sasha to the grill, and took a tired, happy Aiden home. She would have to deal with a sugar buzz for the next week or so, but tonight he dutifully brushed his teeth and went right to sleep. She called Frank—her *fiancé*—but he didn't pick up. She turned on the TV to be sure he wasn't part of breaking news before she went to bed too. She took off her engagement ring, which still felt a little foreign to her, and left it on the nightstand.

****

Friday night Frank called to say, "I love you," but was too busy to talk long. She tried not to worry about him being in danger, and wondered if she had what it took to be a cop's wife. Again she turned on the news to be sure a SWAT standoff wasn't underway, but nothing significant was happening in Powell City. In Cougar, however, a young woman was missing. Twenty-two-year-old Elle Goodman had been babysitting for an infant on Halloween while the parents took their older children trick-or-treating. She left their house before nine o'clock and never arrived home.

Teresa didn't know her, but her surname suggested she was related to two girls she had gone to school with. If the murder in Yaholo had shaken her faith in the safety of small towns, this shattered it. She told herself the missing woman might show up at any minute. Her apparent disappearance might be a misunderstanding or a voluntary absence, but following so soon after the Yaholo incident it was decidedly creepy. She couldn't help remembering Frank's warning about letting Chelsea bicycle home alone after dark. She didn't think she was likely to do so again. She locked both doors, which she almost never did, and made sure all the windows were closed and latched. She felt very vulnerable here, a woman alone with a child. It was comforting to remember she would soon have a man to protect her.

The mystery deepened as the weekend went on. Missing posters hung in store windows when she took Aiden to Sunday school, but nobody came forward to say they had seen the girl Halloween night or since. Nobody remembered seeing anyone suspicious in town. No clues could be found.

She didn't think Aiden had even noticed the posters, but when they got home, he asked, "Bad man kill her? Sasha say—"

"Sweetie, you know Sasha makes things up. Nobody knows what happened. Maybe she ran away."

"Why?"

"I don't know. Maybe she was mad about something or maybe she wanted to go somewhere by herself—alone. Maybe she forgot to tell her mother where she was going. You would never do that, would you?"

"No," he promised stoutly, and then, "Or maybe a bad man took her."

Chapter 15

Monday morning she was putting T-shirts away in Aiden's drawers when the doorbell rang. She was pretty sure she knew who it was before she opened the door and didn't bother to check. He was wearing jeans and a collared shirt with a dark pullover. He looked great. "Hello, Frank," she said, trying to sound casual.

He looked her up and down and whistled, although her hair was tied back in a sloppy ponytail and she wore faded jeans and a pink *Soccer Mom* T-shirt. "That's cute," he said, pointing to the shirt. "Take it off."

Teresa put one hand on her hip—her left, with the third finger in plain view. "Slow down, Frank. You haven't even said hello."

"Hello, Teresa. Take off your shirt."

"I will if you will," she said.

****

"Now I'll have to wash the sheets again," she complained.

"I said I would help with the laundry." He raised himself on one elbow and looked down at her. "You really got into it, didn't you?" he said admiringly. "You're the gift that keeps on giving. It just gets better and better. We're a great match, aren't we?"

"We are," she admitted.

He kissed her. "You taste good, and you smell like…"

"Fabric softener," she supplied helpfully.

While the old washing machine sloshed and gurgled its way through the cycles, they sat at the kitchen table and drank coffee, as she often did with Alix. It was a whole different vibe with Frank, but she tried to keep the same casual tone.

"So," he said, nodding at her shirt. "Aiden plays soccer?"

"He does. At his age, it's pretty much chaos, but they have fun."

"Is he any good?"

"Surprisingly, yes. He didn't get it from me. It's one of the things he's absolutely fearless about."

"Have you thought any more about the wedding?" he asked.

"Instead of wedding plans, we should talk about more practical matters. I have no idea what you'll be like to live with."

He spread his hands. "What you see is what you get. I have no secrets. I don't snore, and I don't leave the cap off the toothpaste. I don't leave my dirty socks on the bathroom floor. What else do you want to know?"

"You're always up. What are you like when you're in a bad mood?"

He shrugged.

"What would you do if I was in a bad mood? Or Aiden?"

"Try to cheer you up, I guess. Chocolate might work for you, right?"

"Chocolate doesn't solve everything—lots of things, but not everything."

"I've seen you in a bad mood. You don't smile. If

it's my fault, I'll apologize. Otherwise, I don't know—introduce you to George Clooney?"

"Do you know George Clooney?"

"No, but it's worth any effort to see you smile."

"Crooked tooth and all?"

"Especially the crooked tooth. You are so damn cute!" He stroked her arm.

"Stop trying to distract me. What about Aiden?"

"You would know best. He probably needs to toughen up a little, but we have plenty of time. I know he's had a hard time so far. After we do the implant—"

"That will be hard too. You can just throw money at the problem, but he'll have to have surgery and work harder than he ever has to make the adjustment. He won't hear perfectly overnight—or ever. You said you didn't expect little boys to man up all the time."

"And I'll never interfere in your decisions about him. I know it's important for parents to be on the same page. When he's ready to accept me completely, I'd like to adopt him, but he'll always be your son first."

"You really are too good to be true, you know."

"What are you doing, Teresa? What is this?"

"I'm trying to solve you, the mystery of you. You have to have a dark side, Frank; everybody does. Alix said—"

He was annoyed. "She doesn't like me," he said.

"That's not true. She doesn't even know you yet, but she thinks you're very attractive. She said you were a catch and if I decided I didn't want you, she would go after you."

Frank was amused. "She's not my type, to say the least."

"What is your type?" she asked.

"You."

"Besides that. What did Nikki look like?"

"Pretty hair, sort of strawberry blonde. She wore it long. Taller than you." He shrugged. "It's getting hard to remember her face, which surprised me at first, but maybe it's natural. You'd start to forget Devlin too, if you didn't keep running into him. I don't like either of us having to see him. The one drawback of living in a small town."

"Yes—I have to see Lacey Norman at least once a week."

"I think that's a little different, isn't it? You were planning to marry Devlin."

"And now I'm going to marry you. Am I too easy, do you think?"

"No, definitely not. Worth the trouble, though." He kissed her.

"Alix said—"

"Enough with Alix. I know she doesn't approve of me."

"That's not true. I told you she thinks you're a catch. She's very supportive. But in the beginning I was concerned that you were going a little fast—and you were—and she said—"

"That I'd abuse you."

"No—just to be careful and to tell you if it was too fast for me."

"Which you did."

"Yes, she gave me good advice."

He was still annoyed, but he took a deep breath and said, "I'm sorry. Your loyalty to your friend is a wonderful thing. I don't want to undermine it. I'm sure she means well, but she might not be the best one for you to listen to. I mean what's *her* relationship history?"

"I don't think that has anything—"

"Okay," he said, with a gesture of appeasement. He was ready to change the subject.

****

Their plans for the weekend began to fall into place, and during one of their nightly phone calls Teresa relayed Aiden's request to invite Sasha to go to the aquarium with them. She was pretty sure Frank didn't like the idea, but he agreed. "Alix should get married again," he said. "Give that girl a father. Somebody needs to take her in hand."

"She might be a little rough around the edges," Teresa acknowledged—but so was Alix. "She's so cute, though. Lots of personality."

"Oh, yeah, she has that," he said and immediately lightened up. Maybe this was his version of a bad mood—get mildly annoyed, deal with it, and then let it go and move on. "You should wear the shirt I bought you," he said, as if he hadn't paid for the ones she chose, too. "Or the thing you wore on the beach."

"I think it will be too cold."

"The T-shirt, then. Don't hide your assets."

"I thought you might like to keep my 'assets' between us."

"I would if you'd share them—are you sure we can't spend the night?"

"No—I mean, yes, I'm sure. I know you like the idea of the three-queen loft room, but I don't think I would be comfortable in bed with you when Aiden could look over the railing, and Sasha is a very light sleeper."

"When we're married…?"

"Aiden knows married people sleep in the same bed."

"Does he understand what Devlin did?"

"I'm sure he doesn't. I don't want him to blame either of us for the breakup…or you. I told him he can like you without being disloyal to Brett and he can still like Brett even if he doesn't see him anymore."

"That would confuse *me*," he said, "but again I'm sure you know best."

****

When she called Alix to invite Sasha, she asked, "Have you had some contact with Frank I don't know about?"

"No, of course not. Like what?"

"I don't know. He seems to have some hostility toward you I don't understand. Like he thinks you don't approve of him or of us being together. I haven't gotten that impression—all you ever did was remind me to be cautious. When I said it was too good to be true, you said there were exceptions to the rule. Right? You don't disapprove, do you?"

"Of course not, kiddo. It looks to me like he's making you happy, and you deserve it. I do think he might be a bit bipolar, but those things are manageable."

"Frank would be pissed if he knew you said that, but he doesn't, so…you never had words with him at the grill or anything? Some reason he'd…"

"No, nothing like that. I've barely spoken to him when you weren't around. You know all there is to know. Did he say something about me?"

"Just kind of maybe I shouldn't listen to you so

much? Like…I don't know."

"Well, you know, Terror, abusers always try to isolate their victims from their friends and family."

"He's not abusive, Alix. He's been nothing but gentle and loving to me. It's downright embarrassing how loving he is. He says Sasha needs a father and maybe you need a man. Could it be you're jealous?" She made it sound like a joke, but they both knew she was serious.

Alix was silent, and then she said, "You'd better think about what you just said, because I don't think you would have ever said that to me before." She hung up.

****

Thursday night after Aiden was asleep, Brett called. In the first weeks after the breakup, she had let his calls go to voicemail and deleted them unheard, but enough time had passed and her circumstances had changed enough that she was able to pick up and calmly say, "Hello."

"I understand congratulations are in order," he said. "I hear you're engaged to this guy and flashing a fancy ring all over town."

"What do you want, Brett?"

"I would have bought you a ring if I knew you wanted one so much, but I had more important things to spend the money on."

"I didn't need a ring. I don't need this one. If you called to berate me, I don't have to listen. I have things to do."

"Sorry," he said. "It's just…I thought what we had was really special until you moved on so fast."

"It wasn't as if I jumped on a dating site. Frank just

happened. I wasn't looking for it. I know the engagement was pretty fast, but...you don't have a right to judge me."

"No," he said curtly. "I guess I have to give up on us now, but I can't give up on Aiden. I have to accept that you'll be with this other guy, this big-shot cop, but if you're over us enough for that, can't you forgive me enough to let me see him? Maybe take him somewhere for a few hours?"

"I don't know, Brett. He's just started to develop a relationship with Frank."

"I don't want to hear about *Frank*. Are you making Aiden hate me?"

"No, not at all. Maybe eventually..."

"If I could have moved as fast as McAllister, if we'd gotten married before all this happened, if I'd adopted him—"

"Or if it hadn't happened at all," she said coldly.

"I'd at least have visitation rights, if not joint custody. I love him, Teresa, like he was my own. I miss him. Please."

Tears made her eyes sting. Gene had never felt as much for Aiden as Brett did. "He misses you too, but..."

"Please."

"Well, maybe..."

"Please, Teresa. I'll do whatever you want—when and where, how long, and you can be there or not be there, whatever you want."

She was definitely weakening. "When?"

He took a quick breath. "Saturday?"

"We're going to the coast. Sunday we're going to the Silver Screen in the afternoon—the Disney thing…Maybe we could meet at the park after church. You know how he loves the swings. I could leave him with you while I do the grocery shopping. You can play and talk for a half hour or so."

"It's a start," he said. "Thank you. I promise you won't regret it."

She already did. "This all depends on Aiden, of course, if he wants to see you. If he doesn't, I can't push it." Reluctantly she added, "Frank won't like it."

"Then don't tell him," he said. He sounded as if he was barely controlling himself. "It's none of his business."

"It will be after we're married."

"There's nothing I can do about that," he said grimly. "After church at the park?"

"Yes. I can't promise anything else."

"Thank you."

She was about to say goodbye and hang up— business done—but instead she said, "Brett? I heard why you got fired. Is it true? You falsified the grant application?"

He hesitated. "No…not exactly."

"You can tell me," she said. "You cheated on me, and I'm still going to let you see Aiden. This won't make any difference."

"I know I screwed things up between us," he said, "but I never stopped loving you."

"That's not what I asked."

"Okay… It wasn't only me. I was the scapegoat." He didn't sound bitter, just wearily matter-of-fact. "Come on, you know how those things work; the school board has to protect itself. Fire me and it all goes away. I wasn't the only one who worked on the proposal.

Several of us did, and it was based on a set of criteria, and it turned out one of them didn't apply. We thought it did; it was an honest mistake at first, but when we found out, we didn't correct it. All of us, not just me. We worked together and reviewed each other's stuff, so we had plenty of chances to speak up, and nobody did. If we had gone ahead without realizing it didn't apply, it would have been nobody's fault, an honest mistake, but we did know. All of us. And somebody blew the whistle. Whoever it was, he or she could have raised objections before we sent in the application, instead of waiting until the money was spent."

"Why did you get blamed?"

"Because I was the one with the best motive. You know, because Aiden benefitted. So the school board decided to cut their losses and can me. It doesn't matter why. Stuff like that happens all the time. Politics."

"But you were a good teacher!" she protested. "Have you had any luck finding another school?"

"No, you know how it is: the economy, budget cuts. A lot of people have gotten pink slips this year. I might be able to get a sub gig in the city now and then."

"I'm sorry. It sounds terribly unfair." She supposed this explanation was self serving and incomplete, but it could be the truth.

"Yeah, well, I did know the proposal was flawed. It's like when you're speeding and you're the only one who gets a ticket—you're still wrong. Anyway, um…it was nice to talk to you. I'll see you Sunday in the park. I'll be waiting."

When she hung up, she decided Brett was right— she didn't have to tell Frank she was letting him see Aiden. She wouldn't lie, but if it came up, she would imply Brett was only babysitting while she did her shopping.

Chapter 16

It was raining when they set out for Genoa on Saturday morning. Aiden and Sasha were at first vastly entertained by the drops racing across the SUV's windows. They liked the comfortable seats, too, and all the novelty of a big, new car, and when the sameness of the passing landscape palled, they sat texting each other and giggling. Frank didn't seem to be bothered by the giggles or Sasha's chattering or the occasional kicks against the seat backs. Aiden was an old soul who had been trained by Teresa to appreciate beauty, so he kept pointing out sights—oddly shaped trees, rain-swollen streams, even the sheen of an oil-streaked highway—to Sasha, who was usually unimpressed.

Despite the gray clouds looming overhead, the view of the ocean at Genoa was spectacular. "Wow!" cried Sasha, who had never seen the ocean before. "Beach water everythere! Golly shakes!"

"Everywhere," Frank corrected automatically and in an aside to Teresa, "Maybe *she* has a hearing problem."

Sasha put a hand on her hip and gave him a saucy look. "I know *where*, Mr. Frank," she said. "It's every*there*!"

Teresa laughed at this logic and said, "She's just a little girl. I think it's cute."

"Yeah, she's cute," he said grudgingly. He had

taken Teresa's hand as soon as they got out of the car. She didn't know what was wrong. He hadn't wanted Sasha along, but didn't seem to mind anything specific.

"It's so good for Aiden to have a friend," she said almost apologetically.

The Oceanfront Aquarium was a hit, as expected. An exhausting amount of juvenile energy was expended while the adults ambled more sedately through the exhibit halls, enjoying the children's enthusiasm as much as they did the sea creatures. It gradually dawned on Teresa that Sasha wasn't the problem; she was. She had done something to displease him, which had seemed almost impossible until now. It didn't make him aloof, though; he kept tight hold of her hand.

While the children giggled in front of the hermit crabs, she asked, "Are you mad at me?"

He was surprised. "No, of course not. For what?"

"I don't know—inviting Sasha?"

"It's fine," he said. "Aiden is happy. That's all that matters."

"Is this what a Frank McAllister bad mood looks like, then?"

"Sorry," he said. "Maybe it's the weather."

"I like this weather," she said. "Rain is beautiful too."

"Right," he said. "Beauty abounds." He smiled and kissed her. "You are so good for me."

Aiden would have been willing to stay all day. If the weather had been better, they would have taken the kids down to the beach, but the rain kept them indoors. The aquarium had its own café, so no restaurant decision was necessary at lunchtime.

A crisis arose when they consulted the menu

posted at the entrance. Sasha wanted ravioli. Teresa chose a veggie burger, and Aiden copied Frank's choice of pizza. Ravioli wasn't on the menu. Sasha didn't want a cheeseburger. She didn't want pizza. She didn't want a chicken sandwich. She didn't want fish and chips. She wanted ravioli. Frank started to say something and then gestured for Teresa to take over. She was the experienced parent here.

"You've been around the Cougar Bar & Grill too long," she told Sasha. "Come on; choose something they have, because if we drive around all day looking for a restaurant that serves ravioli, we may not find one. Fish is the specialty in this part of the world."

"I don't like fish. I want ravioli." She didn't cry. She didn't yell. She didn't stomp her feet. She simply stood in the doorway, wanting ravioli.

"Okay," Frank said. "I'll make you some ravioli. Come on." He directed them to a table for four and went to the counter to put in their order.

"Are you a magician?" Teresa asked when he came back with a numbered marker to set on the table. He just smiled. He handed out drink cups and pointed out the machine that dispensed a variety of beverages. Aiden and Sasha ran over and filled their cups. They could barely reach the levers and created quite a bit of spillage, but very little ended up on the floor. "What are you up to?" Teresa asked.

He was watching the children. "This is what it will be like to have a daughter," he said.

"No, you know what it's really like? I'll get fat and cranky, and we won't be able to have sex for weeks, and the baby will keep us awake at night…"

"I'm up for all of it," he said, "if it's with you."

"If you did have a daughter, you'd probably spoil her."

"I don't believe in spoiling children."

"You spoil me." He half rose to lean across the table and kiss her, not caring who saw. Aiden and Sasha came back with their drinks, a mixture of their own devising, with fruit punch predominating and plenty of carbonation. Teresa had seen little cartons of milk behind the counter, but didn't push.

Frank got up and took their cups. "What would you like?" he asked her.

"Anything. Sprite or Seven-Up, if they have it."

He came back with Sprite for her and Coke for himself, just as the server delivered the tray with their order. It held Teresa's veggie burger and three plates of hot, cheesy pizza.

"That's not ravioli," Sasha said mutinously.

"I know," Frank said calmly. "I haven't made it yet." He put two pieces of pizza on one plate for himself and the empty plate in front of the little girl. Aiden took his, and Frank asked him, "What's the sign for pizza?" He demonstrated, and Frank copied him. It took more than one try, and he took his time, while Sasha waited, not very patiently. When he was satisfied, he turned his attention back to her. "Close your eyes," he said. She closed her eyes. "Okay. What's in ravioli again?"

"Ravioli," Sasha said.

"Pasta, right? Tomato sauce? Cheese—do you like cheese ravioli?"

"Yes."

"Good, because cheese ravioli is my specialty." He took a small piece of the soft point of a triangle of crust and folded it over the cheese and tomato sauce. "Open your mouth, but keep your eyes closed, or the magic might not work." Sasha opened her mouth, and he popped the bite of pizza in. "What's that?" he asked.

"Ravioli," she said.

"Right." He put the rest of the piece of pizza on her plate. "You can open your eyes now."

She opened her eyes, still chewing the morsel. Teresa and Aiden laughed at the expression on her face. "Pizza," she said accusingly, realizing she'd been hoodwinked.

"Ravioli," Frank said, pointing. Teresa finger-spelled the word for Aiden.

"Nunh-uh!"

"Looks like ravioli to me. Pasta, cheese, tomato sauce. Voilà, ravioli."

"Nunh-uh," she said again, but with less heat. "Crust isn't pasta. It's pizza."

"Ravioli," he said persuasively. He smiled at her as if they shared an inside joke. Teresa almost held her breath, but he was completely calm and patient.

Sasha hesitated. She picked up the piece of pizza and took a bite. "Ravioli," she repeated, only slightly wistful. Teresa clapped, and Aiden followed her lead.

"Good girl," Frank said. The charmer had another conquest. He took a bite of pizza and then pulled out his phone and texted something to Aiden that made him laugh. Teresa didn't want him to use his phone as a substitute for personal interaction, but so far he was keeping a pretty good balance.

After lunch, Frank took Aiden to the restroom, and Teresa and Sasha went to the ladies' room. While they washed their hands, Sasha splashing a bit, Teresa asked her if she wanted to go to the movie with them the next day. She didn't think Frank would mind, because the kids could entertain each other. She had taken her before and knew she could behave well enough. "I already saw it," Sasha said. "It was stoopid."

"Don't tell Aiden that."

"Oh, he'll like it," she said confidently. "He's a *boy.*"

Teresa couldn't help laughing. "Strange creatures, aren't they?"

When the kids had—finally!—had their fill of the aquarium, they visited the gift shop, where Frank bought Aiden a toy shark like the one he had wanted to buy at Oxhead, and Sasha picked out a starfish necklace. The rain had stopped, but it was still too cold to stay out long, so they took a quick walk on the beach, found a candy store, and headed for home.

****

When Sasha had been delivered to Alix, they took a tired and happy Aiden home. Frank stayed for dinner. It was her first opportunity to cook for him, and she had a little taste of first-date nerves but was pretty confident now, both about their relationship and about her own abilities. Because they had eaten junk food at lunch and saltwater taffy on the way home, she concentrated on good nutrition. She poured milk even for Frank, because it would set a good example for Aiden. She gave him a look to warn him not to protest, but he didn't seem to need it. Aiden was teaching him signs— *milk, chicken, carrot, beans, tomato, bread.*

"Your mom's a good cook too," he said after he tasted the chicken. "And here I thought she was only pretty to look at."

Aiden shrugged. "She don't make pizza."

"Doesn't," Teresa said.

"How about ravioli?" Frank asked, and Aiden giggled at the good joke they had played on Sasha.

"Not from scratch," she said, "but I'm very good with a can opener." She reflected that if she gave up her job, he would expect her to cook like this every night. She would have to expand her recipe file. Did she want to quit her job? Did she want to be a stay-at-home mom? He was right; it would be better for Aiden, especially if they had a lengthy ordeal with the cochlear implant. But what about her independence—was she ready to give it up for financial support and good sex? The latter might not even last. He didn't believe the honeymoon phase would end, but it always did.

He didn't seem to want to leave. They played Crazy Eights and watched the Disney Channel, and then Teresa sent Aiden in to take his bath—he had recently graduated to doing it all on his own—and finally tucked him in with a goodnight kiss. "Did you have fun today?"

"Yes. Can I have hermit crab?"

"We'll see," she said. "We would need an aquarium." She sketched the size she meant in the air, not to suggest something like the Oceanfront. He would be seven soon, old enough to begin having the responsibility of a pet. She wouldn't have considered incurring the expense before Frank came into her life. I cannot be bought, she reminded herself.

When she came back to the living room, he had the remote and was flipping through channels, but he turned the TV off and opened his arms for her to come and sit close to him. She was glad enough to get off her feet and snuggle up to him. "Are you trying to stay all night?" she asked.

"Uh-huh." He kissed her.

"It's not a good idea."

"Yes, it is." They kissed for a long time. "How long does it take for Aiden to fall asleep?"

"Not long. He'll be out like a light any minute if he's not overexcited from today."

"It was fun, wasn't it?"

"Yes, it was. Thank you."

"It wasn't all me," he reminded her.

"No, but you paid for everything, and you were so good with the kids."

"I knew Sasha just needed handling," he said.

"Uh-huh, and you know how to handle the female of the species, don't you?"

"I know how to handle this one, anyway," he said, and his hand slipped under her shirt. She hadn't worn the one he'd suggested because the weather was too cold for it, opting instead for the long-sleeved navy T-shirt with the lighthouse design, which he had also paid for.

"You do," she admitted, "but it's bad for you to get your way all the time."

"Is it?" He kissed her, cradling her head on one arm while the other hand crept under the band of her bra.

When she could breathe, she asked, "Exactly what are you trying to accomplish here?" She was teasing, flirting a bit, but she was also serious. He was unusually intent today, possessive in a new way. He had held her hand almost continuously in the aquarium.

"Staking my claim," he said in much the same tone

she had used.

Teresa held up her left hand, making the diamonds sparkle. "I think you've already done that."

"I need to make sure of you," he said. They kissed for a few more minutes, and Teresa was enjoying it more all the time. "Let's adjourn to the bedroom," he said.

"No, Frank."

"Yes."

"So you can 'stake your claim'?"

"Yes."

"What's in it for me?" she joked.

He straightened, took her hand, and started to get up. "Allow me to demonstrate," he said.

Teresa laughed and allowed herself to be helped up and led into her bedroom. He started to close the door, and she said, "I never close it." He hesitated and then went ahead and closed it. He didn't lock it. She didn't think Aiden would get up, but she hoped he would know enough to knock first if he did.

Frank pulled her T-shirt off, not without help, and knelt to take off her shoes and jeans. He eased her back on the pillows and kissed her until she was breathless. She had not anticipated this and was wearing her least sexy underwear. He took them off, the bra too this time, and then he gave her the best oral sex of her life—not that the bar had been set very high.

"So far so good?" he asked, while she was still trying to catch her breath.

"Yes," she managed to whisper. He smiled and stroked her face and then moved down to her breasts. "I love you," she said.

"You only say so in bed," he pointed out.

"I guess we'll have to keep doing this, then," she said. She didn't have an excuse and didn't know what else to say. He proceeded without further comment and "staked his claim" in no uncertain terms, again holding her wrists at the end. She didn't think about whether she was bothered by it or not; it didn't last very long, and she had other things on her mind.

"Well?" he asked.

Teresa smiled up at him. "I'm not going anywhere."

"Are you sure?" Did he sense her uncertainty about giving up her independence, or perhaps the slight guilt she felt for not telling him about Brett's call?

"I'm sure," she said. "Do we need to have a talk about jealousy and possessiveness?"

"No," he said. "I think we're good."

"I thought when you bought me a sexy shirt you must not mind if other guys look." Had that been her idea or Alix's?

"Not if they know you're mine. I like to show you off a little."

They lay in bed for a while longer and played a game of "Have you ever?" which proved they were more alike than they had supposed—he was more conventional than she'd thought, and she was less so than he'd expected. All too soon, she made herself get out of bed and put her clothes back on. "No, you can't stay all night," she said before he could ask.

He got up and reached for his pants. "Breakfast?" he asked.

"No!" she said, laughing. "Every time I try to draw a line, you try to blur it. I need to go to bed at a decent hour and get up and make pancakes."

"I like pancakes."

"Another time. We're going to church and grocery shopping, and we'll be waiting here with bells on for you to pick us up for the movie." She kissed him. "Okay?"

"With bells on?"

"Ready to enjoy ourselves—I believe that's the meaning."

"I'd like to see you in literal bells," he said. "Just the bells."

She laughed again. "Go home, Frank. Tomorrow will be here before you know it."

After he was gone, she double-checked the windows and locked both doors. Elle Goodman had still not been found—forty-eight hours now, and no sign of her or her car. Scary.

Chapter 17

The time they got out of church could vary, and it was on the early side today, but Brett had said he would be waiting, and she knew he would be. He was early for almost everything. She felt a little guilty about not telling Frank, when they had agreed to no bullshit, especially because she now wore his expensive ring. It wasn't a lie, but a sin of omission. Sometime in the future, when he was surer of his place in her life, she would at least tell him Brett's version of the falsified grant proposal. It wasn't as if she was having a tryst; she would speak to him briefly and leave Aiden with him for a little while. If Aiden balked, she would be sorry, but also relieved.

The park was located on a grassy hillock alongside the public library and a block from the Silver Screen. It held only swings, a sandbox, a slide, and a small duck pond, but was a popular place for library patrons to take their kids. They were almost to the movie theater when Aiden, looking out the window, cried, "Frank!" Surprised, Teresa saw the Acura parked in the theater lot. He was standing beside the car, looking up, his head back, and holding a handkerchief to his face. She glimpsed blood and immediately pulled over, half across the sidewalk, not taking the time to maneuver into a parking place.

"Stay in the pickup," she told Aiden, who was

already half unbuckled. She got out, and Frank turned and saw her. Blood had spattered the front of his shirt. "What happened?" she asked. "Did you have an accident?" She glanced at the SUV but didn't see a crumpled fender or cracked windshield. A more dramatic possibility leapt to her mind—this was a symptom of some dreadful disease, and his rush to marry her was because he didn't know how long he had to live. Not a Hallmark movie—a Nicholas Sparks novel.

He took the handkerchief away. "Your old boyfriend gave me a bloody nose," he said. It didn't look bad, a little pink and slightly swollen, probably not broken.

Her first, instinctive thought was, Did you hurt him? Instead she took a breath and said, "Are you okay? I thought you were trained in self defense."

"Ha, ha," he said humorlessly. "It was a fluke." He dabbed at his nose again and said, "I think it's stopped."

Teresa found a moist wipe in her purse and gave it to him. "What happened? What are you even doing here? The movie isn't for hours."

Instead of answering, he looked down and said, "I'd better go home and change my shirt."

"Put ice on your nose," she advised. She waited for an explanation, but none was forthcoming. He didn't ask why she was there, either. He knew she was going grocery shopping, and the Supermart was only three blocks away. Maybe he needed to shop too, or had hoped to run into them. She kissed his cheek, an awkward, comforting kiss, trying not to hurt him, and at the same time her face flushed with heat as she remembered last night, emotion heightened by this unlikely surprise.

Frank waved her away and got back in his car. She would have waited a little longer, but her pickup was in the way. She got in and buckled up. "Nosebleed," she signed, checked for traffic, and backed into the street.

Aiden's nose was pressed to the window. He didn't seem upset—he knew a thing or two about nosebleeds. Teresa did her best to remain calm and matter-of-fact for him, but inside she was furious. She did have to have a talk with Frank about this stupid, unreasonable jealousy.

She found a parking place near the swings and waited for Aiden to climb out before she looked for Brett. She was half anxious, half dreading to see him. Aiden saw him first. He ran to him and hugged him tight. Brett's hand was gentle on the boy's hair, but when he raised his head he looked shocked and indignant. "Teresa," he said, tight-lipped. There were tiny spots of blood on his shirt and even on his glasses, but he seemed unhurt.

"I saw Frank," she said inadequately. "I'm sorry, but I don't know if I can leave Aiden with you if you're going to go around hitting people."

"He provoked me!" She didn't doubt it. Brett wasn't easily angered. He was more likely to grow silent, morose—"sulking," she had teased him. He hadn't even been angry about being fired—sad, hurt, not angry—but it was easy enough where Frank was concerned.

"There's no excuse for assault," she said coolly. She touched Aiden's shoulder, and he let go of Brett and turned to her. "Go swing for a minute while we talk." He went, dragging a little, sat down in a swing, gave himself a halfhearted push, and then sat watching them. Brett looked at the ground, silent but seething. "It doesn't look like he hit you back," she said.

"No."

"You need to clean your glasses, though."

He took them off, rubbed the lenses with his handkerchief, and put them back on before he met her eyes. "Teresa, he said some pretty ugly things to me—about you, that you belonged to him, and he was pretty graphic. Damn! He was *trying* to provoke me, and I let him."

"What do you mean? What did he say?" She couldn't imagine what he could have said, what he would have said.

He shook his head. "He said to stay away from you and Aiden."

"What did he say? About me?" He shook his head again. "What did he say to make you hit him? He could file charges for assault!"

"He said he would if I contacted you again. He said—" Brett looked away, distressed, and the words came out in a rush: "He said 'her sweet little pussy belongs to me now' and…what he would do to you."

Teresa felt as if she had been slapped. It didn't sound like Frank, and yet it did—*your body is so responsive, so sweet all over.* She didn't think Brett could have made it up—not the awkward, tentative man she had known, always embarrassed when they had to discuss personal things like her period, sex, or birth control.

"That's not the way you talk about a woman you love," he said indignantly. "That's not love! God! Love is supposed to make you happy, and I'm in hell, and you—are *you* happy, Reesie? With that man? He's a bully. I don't want him around my son!"

"He's not—"

"I mean *your* son." He was a little flustered now over his Freudian slip. She knew he did love him like a son. "He said if I bothered you or Aiden ever again, he would get me fired from the orchard too." He glanced toward the swings and gave Aiden a little wave and a half smile, and Aiden, reassured, began to swing again, gently, still watching. Brett took a deep breath, and they both stood there with nothing to say. She felt the way she had after Frank put the handcuffs on her: not feeling anything, stunned into silence, with no idea what to say. Brett ran a hand through his hair. "What I don't get is why you told him," he said.

"Told him what?"

"That I'd be here, that we were meeting here."

"I didn't," she said.

"You must have."

"But I *didn't.* I should have, but I knew it would upset him, and I didn't think he needed to know."

He shook his head. "He didn't happen by and see me. He was *searching* for me. I was over by the library, and he was looking around for me. And he said the same words I did—visitation, joint custody, that it would never happen. You really didn't tell him?" She shook her head. "Who *did* you tell? Somebody told him what I said."

"Nobody, not even Alix. I didn't have time. I don't think she would have talked to him anyway—he doesn't like her." She didn't mention that Alix might not be speaking to her now, although she had been cordial enough when they picked up Sasha and brought her home. Brett stared at her, mystified. She thought back, trying to remember what had been said and when. Nobody was around when she'd talked to him on the phone, not even Aiden, who was asleep and couldn't have heard anyway. "I didn't talk about it to anybody but you. You called me—Frank wasn't with me."

He took a deep breath. "Let me see your phone," he said. She didn't see why, but she got it out and handed it to him. Who was he going to call? "Oh!" he said. "This is yours? It's pretty flashy."

"Frank bought it for me."

"Did he have access to it?"

"What do you mean? He bought it. He set it up for me."

He touched keys, looked at the screen, and then took a step back from her, even more shocked than he had been when she came. She couldn't imagine what he was looking at—surely Frank wouldn't sext her. He hadn't had the phone to take pictures of her—unless it was while she was asleep. Brett turned off the phone, opened something on it, took out the battery, and threw it away, toward the sandbox.

"What are you doing!?"

It took him a minute to get words out. "There is an app on your phone. It's what they call a boyfriend app. It's to track you. He can use it to listen to your phone calls and read your texts."

She had never heard of such a thing. She shook her head. "That's impossible. It can't be legal."

"Not without your permission it isn't. He could even make your phone call his number if he wanted and listen to you when you're not on the phone, eavesdrop on all your conversations. It's not legal to do it without your knowledge. You should take it to the police."

"He *is* the police," she said bleakly. She was wearing a long-sleeved T-shirt and a denim jacket, and the weather was mild enough, but she was chilled to the bone.

A dozen things were thrown into sharp relief. His mood the day before, a little grim and then persistent, possessive, needing to stake his claim—*after* her conversation with Brett. What he had said about thinking she was married—"you have to push through the hard stuff and do whatever is necessary." Brett saying, "he would get me fired from the orchard *too*"— was Frank the whistleblower?

All the conversations she had had on the phone with Alix, discussing him and their relationship. His hostility to her best friend—was it after Alix theorized that he was mentally ill or might be an abuser? He knew she would be at the grill the first time he had joined them—he said she had mentioned it, but she didn't think she had, not to him.

He had been talking to Lacey at the bar—could he have set that up as well? Urged Lacey to "console" Brett?

No, this was paranoia, but he *had* proved himself jealous and controlling.

She retrieved the battery and put it in her pocket. "What are you going to do?" Brett asked. She held out her hand, and he gave her the phone. It wasn't until then that she decided she wouldn't return anything to Frank. She wouldn't confront him.

"I'm not going to the police," she said, "but I'll keep it in case I need it to get a restraining order. Can I borrow your phone for a minute?" She put hers in her purse, and while he was taking his out, she took off the ring, the amazing, perfect, channel-set band with its center diamond flashing in the sunlight, and threw it into the duck pond. She knew it might choke a duckling, but she didn't care. She would have liked to throw the phone in, too, and pretend it had never existed.

She dialed Frank's number. She didn't wait for him to say anything, but spoke as soon as he picked up. "It's over. I'm taking Aiden to the movie by myself. Don't come near us, or I'll get a restraining order."

Brett looked as if her words eased something in him, but all he said was, "Good."

"He gave Aiden one, too," she said. "So he could text me and Sasha. It's not this sophisticated, but could you check it?"

"Of course. Are you going to let him stay?"

"Yes, if he wants to." She signed to Aiden, "Stay with Brett or go to store with me?"

He signed back, "Brett," and she turned to go and then stopped.

"Thank you," she said to Brett. "I'm sorry."

When she looked back from the door of the pickup, he was squatting in front of Aiden, smiling and signing. He stood up and went behind him to push the swing, higher than she would, as high as Aiden could want, the boy's face lit up with the joy of a simple, uncomplicated pleasure. Her heart caught in her throat at the stark beauty of the moment.

She shopped on autopilot, not sure what she was buying or what she needed. When she came back to the park, Aiden parted casually from Brett and came running to her, talking and signing eagerly. In the car, she let him talk, glad she couldn't respond while she drove. At home she put away groceries, made a light lunch they could supplement with movie popcorn, ate mechanically, tasting nothing, and kept a casual demeanor for Aiden. She told him Frank couldn't go to the movie with them after all because of his nosebleed—he had to lie down and take it easy, so it wouldn't start again.

She didn't enjoy the movie. She still wasn't feeling much, but thoughts crowded into her mind without order or logic, some practical, some verging on hysteria. Aiden said Brett liked his phone, so he must have checked it. She couldn't take it away until she could figure out if she could afford to replace it. She could revert to her old, simpler phone and her old plan, which she hadn't cancelled yet. There would be no wedding, no home with Frank, no online classes, no baby, no cochlear implant.

Alix was right. He was an abuser. This was abuse. If he was mentally ill, bipolar or whatever, it was no excuse. He was a police officer. He knew it was wrong. If he could be this controlling, what else might he be capable of, even worse than this? He wanted to tie her up. He had pressed to meet Aiden right away. What if he was a child molester, courting a single mother to get to her child, grooming him, flirting with Sasha? Was he stupid enough to think Aiden wouldn't tell? She was too numb even to feel the horror of these thoughts.

He was charming, but his charm was a sham, not to be trusted. He was fantastic in bed, and what was she supposed to feel about that now? About any of this? Alix said abusers would isolate their victims. He wanted to meet her parents, but so far didn't know any of her family or friends, other than Alix and Sasha, and she didn't know his. She had never met a single one of his friends. Did he hang out in the cop bar he had mentioned?

His work hours were very irregular. She didn't know where he was Halloween night, when Elle Goodman disappeared. He helped find the third body at Big Devil Creek—and she had no reason to think the two cases were connected. His wife's death was ruled accidental, but why was an inquest needed in the first place? It was ridiculous to entertain such thoughts. What did his betrayal of her have to do with murder? He had never been rough with her, never more forceful than she could handle.

Boyfriend app. It had a name. It was legal, according to Brett, with permission. Would it be too humiliating to ask Hal Knight if it was true? Who would give permission for such a thing? Cowed women willing to give up privacy to a jealous mate? If people could buy it and use it legally, could it really be wrong? What made it so terrible? What was worse—that she had trusted him or that she had said foolish things and felt exposed?

And in the next breath she knew it was an appalling thing to do, beyond comprehension in its cruel, mocking failure to trust. She *had* kept a secret from him, and he had found it out anyway, in this sneaky, underhanded way. If she had told him in the first place, asked him to understand, defused his anger instead of compounding it with her secrecy, it might even have drawn them closer. He had failed to trust. She had failed to trust.

How self-righteous it seemed now for her to be so

hard on Brett for a single act of infidelity on a night when he drank too much because he had been fired and couldn't tell her why. He had made her feel disrespected. She had rejected him. She had been seduced by Frank. Brett had been seduced by Lacey, but he had done it while committed to her. He was in the wrong, but he had yielded to temptation in a moment of heightened emotion, and she had walked right into it with her eyes wide open.

Why did Frank go to the park to confront Brett when he knew she and Aiden would be on the way? He didn't know what time she would get out of church; she hadn't known for sure herself. Brett had said on the phone he would be waiting, and perhaps Frank had thought he would be early enough and be gone before they arrived—and he nearly had. But he had known since Friday night what had passed between them. Had he been waiting on Saturday for her to say something and decided only later to take action? Why not go to Brett's place instead? Maybe he didn't know where he lived—she wasn't sure *she* knew now. He had said "the orchard," but she had told him that much; he might not know which one.

Why didn't he hit Brett back? He could have, but he wouldn't be able to prove Brett had thrown the first punch. She could not picture Brett doing such a thing! He admitted he had, but it was impossible to imagine. Maybe she didn't know him as well as she supposed.

Aiden enjoyed the movie, not to mention the buttery popcorn, but he hadn't understood everything, and she couldn't answer all his questions because she hadn't paid enough attention. Her negligence didn't seem to bother him much. She remembered when she was his age, seeing the world as so full of mysteries, never more than half understood, that any single unanswered question was not very important. Maybe it was more so for him, when he was so often unable to understand the conversation around him. What did the motives of animated characters matter when Mama kept changing father figures on him? He was so curious, so intelligent, and she was a bad mother to allow herself to be distracted from helping him negotiate a frustrating world.

He was happy tonight, full of energy, splashing in his bath, laughing at *America's Funniest Home Videos.* He was glad to have seen Brett again, and although Brett hadn't promised anything, he had left Aiden with the sense that they could meet again before too long. To distract herself more than him, she asked what he wanted to do for his upcoming seventh birthday, and later couldn't even remember his answer. Their ritual of reading a story together before bed had now evolved into him reading to her, but she had no idea what he was reading.

As soon as he was down for the night, she called the Cougar Bar & Grill and asked for Alix. "I know you're busy," she said, "but I wanted to be sure you still want us to come over tomorrow. I need to talk."

"Yes, of course," Alix said without hesitation.

Chapter 18

Teresa had to work on Veteran's Day, but it was a school holiday, so as soon as the breakfast dishes were done, she and Aiden went to visit Alix and Sasha. Sasha came running out and took Aiden into the back yard to play, so she climbed the steps alone. The Stars and Stripes was flying from a bracket next to the door, as always on patriotic holidays. Alix was proud to display the flag that had been draped on her husband's casket. When she opened the door, Teresa managed not to do anything as dramatic as burst into tears, but she did give her a hug and get a bit teary. "I'm so glad you're not mad at me."

"Why would I be mad?"

"I said something about you being jealous, and I wasn't sure we parted friends."

Alix waved that away. "It'll always be me and you, kiddo. Men come and go, but women stick together."

"I broke up with Frank," she said abruptly.

"Oh, my God!" Alix grabbed her left hand. "Did you give back the beautiful ring?"

"Worse. I threw it in the duck pond."

"The duck—Well, shit, girl! It isn't very deep. Make him fish the damn thing out and crawl on his hands and knees to give it back to you. I know, power trips aren't your thing, but *I* would. What did he do? You didn't snag another cheater, did you?"

"No," Teresa said. "I'm getting very good at breaking up with guys, though."

"Come on, give," Alix said. They went into the kitchen, where she had been folding laundry. "Here—I'll let you help. I love folding little kid clothes, don't you? They're so cute. When Sasha stops being cute, I'll make her do her own laundry."

"When she stops being cute, you'll borrow her clothes." She folded a pair of Sasha's jeans, still warm from the dryer, and then said abruptly, shakily, "Alix, he put something on my phone to track me."

"Say what? Frank did? Like a GPS thing?"

"Worse. Brett said it was an app that lets him listen to my phone calls and maybe listen even when I'm not on the phone."

"Like a bug? Whoa—could your place be bugged?"

"No, of course not."

"The dude is a cop."

"He's SWAT; he doesn't work with surveillance equipment. You're making me paranoid now. He was in the house one whole evening—I couldn't get him to leave—and he was alone while I tucked Aiden in. But why would he bother if he already had the phone app? It was easier and probably cheaper, and apparently it's legal."

"To bug your phone?" Alix raised her eyebrows.

"With my permission, which he didn't have."

"Well, I'm glad your place isn't bugged, 'cause I enjoy our heart-to-hearts. Tell me what happened. Wait—did you say Brett said? You've seen him?"

She waved her hand to show it wasn't significant. "I let him see Aiden, and Frank knew where we were meeting; that's how we discovered it. And Brett gave him a bloody nose!"

Alix's mouth dropped open. "Clark Kent hit Superman?"

Teresa gave a shaky laugh. "Something like that," she said.

"So you chucked the ring in the pond and told Frank to skedaddle? When was this?"

"Yesterday after church."

"Have you heard from him since?"

She shook her head.

"Well, he's a man. He can't deal with emotional women, so he'll give you a few days to cool off. Are you going to forgive him, or are you done?"

"He listened to my private conversations! He's what you said, an abuser, trying to isolate and control me. How can I forgive him? I don't think I can even look at him."

"Good for you," Alix said approvingly. She smiled at the nightgown she was folding. "Little girl clothes are prettier, but sometimes I wish I'd had a boy. So...you didn't get yourself pregnant, did you?"

"No, we used protection, except the first time."

"And I know you can count."

"It was all bullshit, wasn't it? 'Oh, Teresa, you're so beautiful.' He just wanted somebody he could control. I probably don't even have pretty feet."

"Oh, yes, you do, Terror! You have all your toes and everything."

"Thanks, pal. And I almost let him come between us. I'll never have anything like this again, will I? My little rebound romance. He was so charming, so seductive, and it was very flattering. What an idiot!"

"Gosh, maybe I should seduce him, get a taste of that."

Teresa laughed without humor. "Just don't let him touch your phone. I only use mine for calls. I'm not even sure what an app *is*."

"Where is it? Do you have it with you? I'd like to give him an earful, 'cause nobody gets away with hurting my BFF."

"I put it in a drawer. It's turned off, and Brett even took the battery out. Did you ever hear of this? He called it a boyfriend app."

"Oh, yeah, it's like they clone your phone or something. He could read your texts—if you texted—and see what websites you visited." Alix gasped. "Do you think he knows we Googled him?"

She shrugged. "I don't know what to think about any of this. It's so wrong, but it never seemed like he was controlling in any obvious way. I mean he had our whole future planned and he told me what to wear a couple of times, but he didn't say anything when I didn't take his suggestion. I don't know—could the app have come with the phone? Could somebody at the phone store have done it?"

"Not if Frank was the one who intercepted your calls—if he knew what you said to Brett. Can I play devil's advocate here for a minute?"

"This is why I like talking to you," Teresa said. "You never take a hard line on anything."

"Okay—from the very beginning, Frank hasn't been a bad guy, just a little overenthusiastic, right? This is an extreme example of the same thing. He's sort of obsessed with you, and he got carried away."

"Are you saying I should forgive him?"

"No, but maybe give him a chance to explain; don't condemn him unheard. If this was a TV plot, it would turn out he suspected you were an international spy and had to keep tabs on you, or—"

Teresa laughed. "You are so good for me," she said.

"Are we sure Brett didn't make up this app thing?"

"How else would Frank know about our conversation? Do you think I'm right to break up with him over this?"

"It's certainly a serious breach of trust. If you did decide to take him back, you would be in a position to dictate whatever terms you wanted."

"But I would never be able to trust him again," Teresa said. "He gave me this great massage in Grey Harbor the first time, and he said no, don't worry about me; it's all about you, blah, blah, blah, like all he wanted to do was make me happy. He made me feel sexy. How could I not have known it wasn't real? Who am I to deserve that?"

"Don't get down on yourself. You deserve all that and more."

"The sex was so great," she said wistfully. "Exciting, challenging. I'll never find anything like it again. I think I'll become a nun."

"Now you get why I could never replace my jarhead. We were so perfectly matched."

Alix so rarely mentioned her husband that Teresa had to busy herself helping her get coffee to keep tears from welling up. By the time they were settled at the kitchen table, she was in an unusually confiding mood.

"The last time," she said, "Saturday night? He— when he was probably pissed at me because I didn't tell him about Brett—he…"

"Come on, give. You know you want to."

Teresa got up and went to the window to make sure Sasha was safely out of hearing. She and Aiden seemed to be chasing each other's shadows. "He, you know…went down on me."

"No shit? Was it good?"

"It was *fabulous*."

"Maybe he wasn't pissed. Maybe he felt threatened and wanted to remind you he was the better man. Brett never did it, did he?"

"No. I mean—can you imagine? Gene did a few times, but it wasn't much. He just wanted *me* to."

"Did Frank?"

"No."

"Brett is a good guy, though, right? Not as exciting maybe, but you were happy with him for a while. He'd be a better father anyway. Is there any possibility of you getting back with him? Sex isn't everything."

"With him it was…comfortable. Safe. I guess it was more at first, and it was lovely for a while." She didn't want to remember that it had been lovely right to the end.

"Lacey didn't have any complaints," Alix said.

"Oh, God, did she talk about him? He would be so embarrassed!" And the way they were talking about him this morning was a betrayal too.

"No, no, she was just, you know, very pleased with herself."

"Yeah, that sounds like her. The best part was the way Brett was with Aiden…" She sipped her coffee and sighed. "Maybe I'm feeling nostalgic because of the mood I'm in now. I'm afraid that ship has sailed, and

I'd better concentrate on going solo. I mean I can't forget he cheated on me." A part of her was filled with regret for what might have been, but she was afraid too much damage had been done.

"Yeah, and how long do you think Frank would have been a faithful husband?"

"Good point. If he didn't trust me, maybe he isn't trustworthy. I read somewhere that men who constantly accuse their wives of cheating secretly want them to—so they can watch."

"Jeez—what have you been reading?"

"I think it was in an Ian McEwan novel. Anyway, I'm glad I decided to let Brett see Aiden. It made them both so happy. Frank was better with him than I expected, though. He said he didn't have any experience with kids, but he did fine. I guess the SWAT hero-worship thing helped."

"He certainly charmed the pants off Sasha."

"Don't even say such things—this shook me up so much it occurred to me he might be a child molester or a serial killer."

"Back to Mary Higgins Clark. Being a controlling son of a bitch doesn't make him a murderer."

"I know, paranoid, huh? It's like if he didn't really love me, he must be crazy. "

"It sounds like you have healthy self-esteem, at least."

"But he didn't have an alibi the night Elle Goodman disappeared—or maybe he did, but I didn't know where he was, and he didn't answer his phone. And there was the thing with his wife."

"Edris." Alix made a face.

"Oh, I didn't tell you; he said she went by Nikki.

We should Google her again."

"Yeah, give me your phone…oh, no, you can't. I'll do it later on my computer. If I turn it on when Sasha's home, she'll play games all day. How is it spelled?"

"He didn't say."

"But he talked about her? What else did he say?"

"Not much. I asked what she looked like. He was talking about his type…" She remembered what he had said—that Alix wasn't—and quickly added, "Let's change the subject. I want to do something special for Aiden's birthday."

"Oh, good. Sasha's making something for him."

"I can't wait to see it. If we have a big party, we can invite Brett without it being weird."

Alix put her hand on Teresa's. "You know, I wanted so much to see you happy, but now we can swear off men together. Women are stronger and smarter than men, and the only reason they have the power is they're physically bigger than we are—and what is that? It's what a bully relies on; it's not real strength."

"Brett said Frank was a bully, but he was so nice to me… Oh, you know what else he said? Brett? He called Aiden 'my son'—accidentally, but I thought it was kind of—" She couldn't say *sweet* anymore.

"We've given up on men, remember? Including Brett. He hit Frank, which makes him a bully too. And how do we know *he* isn't a child molester or a serial killer? Does he have an alibi for Halloween?"

"Yeah, well…he's a dope anyway."

"That's the spirit." The back door banged open, and the children came in. Their cheeks were flushed with exertion in the cold air, which followed them in.

"Close the door!" Alix snapped. "Were you raised in a barn?" Sasha gestured to Aiden, and he slammed the door. "Did it start raining?" It had been threatening all morning.

"No," Sasha said and then announced indignantly, "Aiden can run faster than me."

"Sasha run like girl," Aiden signed. Teresa didn't know where he had learned that—not from her. If he had picked it up at school, at least he was interacting with other boys.

"Yeah, boys are better at a few things, you know," Alix said. "Not many, but a few." She winked at Teresa. "While you're in here, take those clothes to your room. If you stay and talk to us, we'll let you help with some other exciting chores. We might even let you do them by yourself! Girls are a lot better at housework."

Sasha signed, "Out," to Aiden, and they ran back outside, slamming the door.

Chapter 19

Frank called for the first time Tuesday morning, when Teresa was at work, hand feeding a ferret recovering from surgery to remove a tumor. She let the call go to voicemail and deleted it unheard, as she had when she wasn't speaking to Brett. He kept calling all day. She couldn't turn off the phone, in case Aiden or the school needed to contact her, but she put it on vibrate and deleted the messages.

She reflected that maybe it hadn't been the best strategy with Brett, but she didn't intend to talk to Frank, especially on the phone. She was clueless enough about technology that she wasn't sure he couldn't plant something on her old phone merely by calling her.

She worried that he might come to the house, so she and Aiden hung out all evening with Alix and Sasha at the grill and went home with them to spend the night. To Aiden it was an unexpected treat. Teresa didn't let him have a hot dog or macaroni and cheese this time, but he was happy with fish tacos. Frank could find her easily enough at the grill, but she would have Alix and some of the regulars on her side.

When the little ones were in bed—hopefully sleeping and not giggling the night away—Alix turned on her computer, and they Googled Nikki McAllister. They found thousands of hits, but the addition of

Frank's name to the search terms narrowed the results to a handful, including a newspaper headline reading "Fatal Sex Game." The article said thirty-six-year-old software designer Edris "Nikki" McAllister's death had been ruled accidental. "McAllister's lifeless body was discovered at their Genoa home by her husband, SWAT officer Frank McAllister, when he returned from duty on August 3rd. She was apparently home alone when she died of autoerotic asphyxiation, the result of a choking game intended to provide a sexual thrill. McAllister was found in bed, partially nude, with a rope around her neck. Friends stated that she was known to experiment with bondage and other unusual sexual practices."

They stared blankly at each other, and then Alix opened Wikipedia and typed in *Autoerotic asphyxiation.* She browsed quickly through the article and read, "No less powerful than cocaine and highly addictive… Deaths often occur…"

Teresa's mouth had gone dry, and she thought her hands might be shaking. "He…he said she got him into the bondage thing," she said. She remembered him saying, "She up and died on me." The words hadn't sounded as cold and accusatory as they seemed now.

"It says flat out she was alone and he found her, not like there was any question. He was on duty, so he had an alibi."

"Unless he snuck away for a little afternoon delight, like he did with me."

"He wasn't a murder suspect, and you know they always look at the spouse first. So…he tied her up, but he wouldn't choke her, so she had to do it herself when he wasn't around? I can see why he left the Genoa PD, once everybody knew about this—I mean, can you imagine?"

"It's so ugly."

"Gross," Alix agreed. "But not his fault. I know how you feel, though. Ick. You must have been like a breath of fresh air to him, Terror. And maybe she cheated on him, so he thought maybe you couldn't be trusted either?"

"I'm just glad I don't have to see him again."

****

He called all day Wednesday, too. *I told you I was the tenacious kind.* Alix invited Teresa to move in, at least for a little while, but they had figured out long ago that they were better as BFFs than as roommates. She reminded the school that only she and Alix were authorized to pick up Aiden, and she told Aiden to tell her if anybody except Sasha texted him—including Brett or Frank.

Wednesday night they were back at home. Aiden was getting ready for bed when his phone rang. She went into his room to tell him it was too late to communicate with Sasha, but then she realized it was not the usual tone for a text. He handed her the phone, and she recognized the number. She couldn't let Frank try to use her son as an intermediary. She smiled reassuringly at him, signed, "Pajamas," and walked out of the room before she took the call.

"Stop calling me," she said fiercely. "If I see this number again, I'll tell the police what you did."

She should have hung up on the shocked silence at the other end, but she was almost too angry to move, and then he said, "What? What are you talking about?" in a tone of such bewilderment that her heart leapt with hope. He didn't do anything. Brett had made it up. Maybe he told him about the meeting and set him up. "Teresa, please. I'm sorry about using Aiden's number to contact you, but you didn't answer yours, and I need to talk to you. I know you were mad because I tangled with Devlin, but I thought you would have cooled off by now. *He* hit *me*."

"He told me what you said, the words you used."

"Which was what? I didn't say anything except I wanted him to leave you alone. Cougar is a small town. We're all going to run into each other now and then, but he needs to know he can't keep bothering you. He pushes my buttons, but no matter what he told you, I didn't lay a hand on him. I think I was pretty polite, considering some of the things he said to me. What did he say I said?"

"I'm not going to repeat it," she said coldly.

"I can imagine what he would have made up. Obviously, it's his word against mine, but—" It sounded so reasonable, so plausible, so much the charming, seductive Frank, but she remembered Brett's shock and fury and the words he'd forced himself to repeat.

"He didn't make it up," she said.

"He must have made up something, or you wouldn't be this angry. You know, I don't even blame him for being a little deranged—he lost you." She realized he didn't know she knew about the app—he thought she had frozen him out for three days because he provoked Brett enough to get his nose bloodied.

"You put something on my phone," she said.

"What do you mean?" He sounded so innocent, so reasonable, but she didn't doubt herself this time.

"You know what I mean," she said sharply. "You know it's illegal, and if you call again, I'll give the phone to Hal Knight."

"Wait!" he said, knowing she was about to hang up. "I'm sorry, but I did it to protect you, to keep you safe. That's why I gave you the phone in the first place, for emergencies."

"To keep me safe?" she echoed derisively. "By invading my privacy, listening to my conversations, spying on me? You did it behind my back. If it was for my protection, you would have told me."

"I'm sorry," he said. "You're right; I should have told you. But you can't throw away what we have because of one misstep." It sounded so familiar—a man she had trusted asking her to forget he had betrayed her. "I love you, Teresa," he said in his caressing, loving, persuasive way. His voice made her tingle, and it was hard to tell if it was anger or arousal.

"Fuck off, Frank," she said and hung up.

****

The weather was cold and gloomy through the weekend, and it rained heavily Saturday night. Teresa wasn't depressed by bad weather; she rather liked it. Rain had its own beauty, and the world would grow greener because of it. She was snug and safe in her little house, listening to the rain on the roof, with her son dreaming his innocent dreams in the next room.

She still locked the doors and windows every night, but she was starting to feel silly about it. That a girl had gone missing from Cougar a few months after another one disappeared from Yaholo didn't mean she was in danger. If anything, it meant she was safer than before—if a serial killer was out there somewhere, he wouldn't be seeking a new victim this soon. She couldn't even be sure Elle Goodman had met with a bad end. Her car was gone too—she could have driven out of town for reasons nobody was yet aware of.

That line of reasoning changed on Monday morning when the *Independent* confirmed what had been a whispered rumor at church the day before: Elle Goodman's body had been found. She had been sexually assaulted, strangled, and her partially clad body buried in a shallow grave at the town dump.

The location of the body suggested the killer was an outsider or someone who hadn't lived in Cougar long. A local would have known the first heavy rain would make the soft earth at the edges of the landfill shift and uncover the body. Now Teresa's fear seemed only too reasonable. She told herself they couldn't assume one person was responsible for both crimes, in spite of the similarities. If it *was* a serial killer, he had taken one victim from Yaholo and one from Cougar—wouldn't he be likely to choose another location next time? In any case, he would know everybody was extra alert right now, extra cautious, so it was the worst possible time.

All of this and more was discussed at length over coffee with Alix before she went to work. In addition to her unease about the murder, she was deeply depressed about her love life. Her anger at Frank had nearly spent itself, and she was sorry the affair had ended so badly. Her relationships always ended badly. Gene, Brett, Frank—three strikes and you're out.

"Now you're starting to get it," Alix said with some satisfaction. "Ninety-nine point nine per cent of the men in the world are not worth the trouble."

"What happens with the other point one per cent?" Teresa asked. "And how do I find them?"

"They die," Alix said starkly.

"Oh, Alix!" Teresa put her hand on her friend's.

"It's true. My advice? Buy a good vibrator and hire a repairman when you need one. What else do we need them for?"

Chapter 20

It wasn't raining when she got off work at seven, but thunderheads had been building on the horizon all day. The moon was just past full, and the sky was bright, but the light was beginning to diffuse behind a thin overcast. The wind was cold, and she was glad to pick Aiden up at Alix's and get home to her space heaters and a hot dinner. She had made a tuna noodle casserole she could pop into the oven while she put together a spinach salad—he would like it if she put enough cucumber in it.

He ate well enough but was a little subdued, and finally he told her what was on his mind: "Bad man killed her." No doubt Sasha had been filling his mind with gory details.

Teresa took a deep breath. "Yes, but don't be scared. I'm sure he's far away now." She wasn't sure, of course. She was a little scared tonight herself, and it made her want a man. Not for sex, but to hold her and make her feel safe and protected. She had had that, but nothing precious could last long. Everything was fleeting, including life itself. Elle Goodman and the young woman from Yaholo had probably believed otherwise, had made plans for their futures, and they had been snuffed out.

By the time Aiden was in bed, thunder was rumbling in the distance, and the moon was hidden. The wind made things outside rattle and bang in unfamiliar, unsettling ways. She searched through her DVD collection, now mostly Brett's choices, for a comedy to cheer and distract her—or would this be the right time for an old-fashioned tearjerker? Maybe what she needed tonight was a good cry.

She decided on *The Untamed Heart.* She could identify with Marisa Tomei, so unlucky in love, and Christian Slater was cute in a completely nonthreatening way. All she needed to make the evening complete was the carton of Breyers triple chocolate ice cream she happened to have in the freezer.

She was settled on the couch with her bowl of ice cream, her slippered feet propped on the coffee table, feeling a little guilty because she wouldn't let Aiden do it, when lightning flashed outside the windows. She counted the seconds before the thunder rolled—it was close, but not frighteningly so. Rain pattered on the awnings. She paused the DVD and went down the hall to check on Aiden, because lightning sometimes scared him.

He was sound asleep, facing toward the window, with his blankets wrapped close around his shoulders against the cold. She bent and left a feather-light kiss on his cheek. As she straightened up, lightning flashed again, and for a split second a shadow moved beyond the curtained window. *Prowler.* The thunder came soon after, but not as loud as before.

She peered out the window, but she couldn't see anything. She went quickly out and closed the door behind her. She turned off the living room light so she could see out and wouldn't present a clear silhouette in the window. Her mind was racing—her phone was in her purse—*call 911—yell "Call 911" so he'll think somebody else is here—what if he tries to break in?—what can I use as a weapon?* She couldn't see anything outside; it was too dark. She waited for another flash of lightning to illuminate the scene, and then she heard a sound on the porch, and her heart banged in her ears.

She scrambled for her purse. Just as her fingers closed on the phone, there was a knock at the door, neither tentative nor demanding. She held her breath. "It's me, babe," a voice called. *What?* It sounded like Frank's voice, but he never called her babe or anything like it. "Open the door," he said, sounding calm, ordinary. "It's raining like hell out here."

She switched on the porch light and opened the door a crack, but kept the chain on. He stood on the porch, dressed in a heavy overcoat, shoulders hunched, trying to shelter in the doorway. The rain was coming down hard now. "Teresa," he said, as if he was happy to see her, as if this was not in any way unusual. "Let me in before I drown."

She was still angry with him, but she was glad to see somebody familiar and not a serial killer. Familiar felt safe tonight. She unhooked the chain and opened the door. She didn't want him in the house, but she didn't want to carry on a conversation through the door in this weather, either. The air that came in with him was cold and fresh with the scent of rain. She didn't try to make him welcome. "What are you doing here?" she asked. She stepped back, keeping an impersonal distance between them.

He ran a hand through his wet hair and shrugged out of his coat, very casual, as if this was all perfectly normal. "We need to talk," he said. "We can work this out."

She didn't offer to take his coat and hang it in the closet. He held it uncertainly, as if he expected her to, and then draped it over the back of the easy chair. "This is kind of a strange time to come by," she said.

"It's kind of now or never, isn't it?" She didn't understand what he meant, but his tone was so reasonable she thought she must have missed something. He made her doubt herself, and she had done a lot of that lately. "Is Aiden asleep?" he asked. She didn't answer, but he continued as if she had. "I didn't think you'd want to discuss it in front of him."

"I don't want to discuss it at all. Nothing you can say will make any difference."

"You know you're breaking that boy's heart," he said. "You couldn't hang onto Devlin, and now you're cutting me loose? He needs a father."

"It's not going to be you."

"I could do so much for him, though. I love you. I think you owe me a chance—"

"What you did was unforgivable."

"I was trying to keep you safe. I have a right to protect what's mine."

"I'm not yours! I was never *yours*. I would have married you, but I still wouldn't have been yours, not that way, not in that tone of voice."

"You belonged to me even before we met," he said. "Come on, admit it: you missed me. Absence makes the heart grow fonder, right?" He smiled, the old charming, persuasive Frank, and put his hands out in a peacemaking gesture. "I'm not here to argue. I'm here to remind you how good it was between us. You can't throw that away."

"Actually, it turns out I can."

He shook his head, amused. "You are so fierce," he said. "But I know you don't mean it. I know you better than you know yourself. Teresa!" His use of her name carried a familiar caressing note, but he was half cajoling, half reproachful. "Come here." She didn't budge, so he came to her, moved closer, not in a threatening way but as if he were approaching a wild thing in need of gentling. Even now, angry and still a little jumpy from the fright she'd had, she could feel the attraction between them. And no, she was not about to be drawn in, suckered again. "I know your body inside and out," he said. "I know you're more adventurous than you pretend to be. I can make you feel so good, and you know it."

"This is not happening, Frank."

"Yes it is," he said and took her arm, gently at first and then more firmly. "Let's go in the bedroom."

"No! You said you wanted to talk."

"We can talk in the bedroom."

"No!" She tried to pull her arm free, but he was too strong for her.

"I have something for you," he said. He reached toward his back pocket. She hadn't told him what she'd done with the engagement ring—surely he didn't intend to replace it? Instead, cold steel snapped closed on her wrist.

"No! Take it off!"

"Calm down," he said. "I know you don't like it, and I'll take it off in a minute, as soon as you go in the bedroom with me. Nothing bad will happen to you, Teresa. Quite the contrary." He didn't wait for a response and maneuvered her toward the hall. She planted her feet and struggled against his hold, but couldn't bring herself to kick or scratch. This was Frank; he would come to his senses in a minute and apologize, as he had at Grey Harbor. She could tell he didn't like her fighting him, but he didn't hit her or shove her or jerk her arm—that wasn't his style. He urged her forward, his fingers on her arm just tight enough, as if he was trying not to bruise her. "You know you want this as much as I do."

But she didn't. He wouldn't kill her, but she was pretty sure she was about to be raped. The irony was that it was a crime she could prevent simply by wanting it to happen, by letting her body respond to his. No coercion, no crime.

If she screamed, who would hear her? Old Mr. Poston next door was nearly as deaf as Aiden. The Doolittles on the other side were visiting relatives out of town. With the wind and rain, her voice wouldn't carry far enough for anybody else to hear. If Aiden had been a hearing child, would she have yelled for him to call 911 or run next door? No—six-year-olds were sound sleepers, and she might have put him in danger.

Frank forced her through her bedroom door and over to the bed, where he fastened the other handcuff to the headboard, making use of those vertical mission-style slats he admired so much. "Relax," he said soothingly. "There's nothing to be afraid of. I'll be right back and take it off." He went out, and she looked around wildly for a way to help herself—a weapon, a phone, something to throw. She could barely reach the drawer of the nightstand and tugged on the handle. Her angle was wrong, so it slid out an inch and stuck and slid again with a squeak.

Frank came back and calmly closed it again. He was carrying two lengths of rope and a knife. Her nerves went taut all over at the sight of the blade. He dropped the rope on the bed, put the knife on the nightstand out of her reach, and went back to close the door. As he did, the brightest flash of lightning she had ever seen lit up the window, immediately followed by an enormous crash of thunder. It shook the whole house. She jumped, and so did Frank, and then he laughed. "That was close," he commented. "Wild night."

"I don't want to do this," she said urgently. "I really am claustrophobic."

"It's all in your mind. The claustrophobia isn't real, not in your case; it's *fear* of claustrophobia." She couldn't deny it; she had used the phrase herself. He tied her free wrist to the top crossbar, undid the handcuff, and replaced it with rope. "That's better, isn't it?"

"I don't want to do it!"

"If you don't like it, we don't have to do it again, but you have to try it this time." His tone was like a parent's, coaxing a reluctant child, like her trying to get Aiden to eat a new vegetable.

"Please, Frank. I don't like this. Please untie me. I'm starting to feel—"

Under her own words and the patter of rain on the awnings, she heard a sound from outside the room, not near the door, but at a distance: a childish treble with the slight harshness common to deafness—Aiden calling, "Mama!" He had probably been awakened by the spectacular lightning and the concussion of the thunder, but she hoped he was only crying out in his sleep.

Frank didn't seem to hear it. "Feeling is what it's all about," he said. "Stop thinking and just feel. What's your philosophy? Beauty abounds? Look for the beauty in this experience. It comes with giving up control."

"I don't want to give up control. If you untie me now, I won't tell anybody."

"I know you won't," he said warmly. "When you wouldn't talk about having sex with Devlin, I knew you could keep a secret." He took hold of her left leg, and she tried to kick him, but he overpowered her and bound both ankles to the footboard. He went to the nightstand and held up the knife. The blade wasn't very long, but had a nasty serrated edge. "The minute we're finished, I'll cut you loose. You're not trapped, so there's no need to be claustrophobic."

"I *feel* trapped."

"Makes your heart race a little? That's adrenaline."

"Is the door locked?" she asked, willing Aiden to stay in bed, out of harm's way. If he opened the door he would be terrified to see her like this, maybe run out in the rain—and what would Frank do?

He held up a finger, as if grateful for the reminder, and went to lock the bedroom door. "I love you," he said.

"This isn't the best way to show it," she said.

"I swear to God I will not hurt you."

"It already hurts," she protested. "The rope is rubbing my wrists. Having my arms up like this is uncomfortable, and the claustrophobia is real; it's no joke."

"You'll forget about it in a minute," he said.

"Pretend you're in Italy. Remember telling me you would let me tie you up if I took you to Italy?"

"Remember me breaking up with you?" she asked.

"I remember you saying something of the kind, but it didn't sound like you. Somebody put those words in your mouth—the bartender, or Devlin." She *was* a little claustrophobic now, jumpy, panicky, trembling, starting to sweat. "I want you to trust me."

"Trust you? Oh, please. Like you trusted me when you put the app on my phone?"

"I guess we'll both have to work on trust issues," he said. He held the knife up again, and she couldn't help a sudden intake of breath.

"You said you wouldn't hurt me," she said. She could barely get enough breath to get the words out.

"That's the last thing I want to do. It's kind of exciting, though, isn't it? Knife at your throat, knowing if I did mean you harm, you would be helpless to resist?" He grabbed the neck of her T-shirt and used the knife to slice through the cloth. It cut easily enough, but the blade snagged in the cotton fabric. "Sorry," he said. "This isn't the best knife for the purpose. I brought it for the rope. It's a pretty shirt, too. I sort of hoped you'd cooperate and we could get you undressed first." She didn't point out that he could have just pulled the T-shirt up. She could see that he was beyond logic now.

He pulled the shirt open and eased his fingers under her bra, caressing and squeezing. When she had thought he would never touch her again, she had made herself forget what his hands could do to her. She remembered now, but instead of arousing her, they made her feel cold and sick. His face was familiar, his hands warm, but he was a stranger now, a predator invading her space. What did he like about this? The snug fabric pressing his fingers into her flesh? The trapped warmth of her breasts? Whatever it was, he took his time. Her arms started to ache.

Teresa took a deep breath and willed herself to relax. She didn't have many options. She couldn't talk him out of it. Her first priority was Aiden. The best way to make him safe was to keep Frank from even thinking about him. Second priority: staying alive. If she let him do what he wanted to do, maybe she could get him to leave afterward. Even if he meant to stay here all night, he would leave before it was time for Aiden to get up.

She would get it over with, and then she would have him arrested. She would get a restraining order. Maybe she would offer to return the favor and tie him to the bed before she called 911. No doubt he would hire a high-priced lawyer, and it would be his word against hers, but she was going to survive this. Whatever happened, she would survive. Nobody ever died from claustrophobia…did they?

Frank checked the ropes around her wrists and then unbuckled his belt and slid it free from the loops. She expected him to lay it aside, and when he instead stretched it between his hands she thought he was going to hit her and flinched. "You said you wouldn't hurt me," she said again.

"Not for the world," he said. "You're safe with me. Now, this part might be a bit scary at first, but it will give you the best experience." He put the belt around her neck and threaded the end through the buckle. Teresa's anxiety level took a quantum leap. Her heart thudded in her chest.

Her mouth was so dry she could barely form

words. "No," was all she could say at first. He tugged experimentally on the loose end of the belt, and Teresa saw stars. The life that flashed before her eyes was not hers but Aiden's. If she died, Gene would have to take him, and they would both hate it. He'd prefer to live with Alix and Sasha, but he wouldn't be allowed to. "Is this what happened to Edris?" she managed to whisper.

"You've been doing your homework," he said. "No, I told you it was an accident. I wasn't even home. If I had been, it wouldn't have ended that way." He sighed. "Nikki was a great girl, lots of fun, but she wasn't very bright. *You* are the love of my life."

"If you love me—" She was too breathless to finish the sentence. *He won't kill me. I have to believe he won't kill me.* The belt wasn't tight at all now, but she could feel the leather and the metal buckle against her skin. "Frank…" She slowed her breathing. *Be still. Don't fight.*

He leaned close and kissed her. "What?"

"I don't want to do it." She tried to speak calmly, but it came out close to a whimper.

"Yes, you do." He sat on the edge of the bed to take off his shoes and then stood up and unzipped his pants. The doorknob rattled, and they both looked in that direction. He took a step toward the door.

Teresa was terrified. They had been in the bedroom long enough that she had hoped Aiden would have gone back to sleep by now. "He got up to go to the bathroom," she said desperately. "He'll go right back to bed." Frank glanced back at her, hesitating. "He can't hear us," she reminded him. They waited and heard only silence on the other side of the door and the wind and rain outside the window.

"Right," he said. He moved back to her and patted her leg in reassurance.

"Don't do it," she said. She thought she might black out even before he could tighten the belt around her neck.

Frank leaned over her, about to straddle her, speaking softly. "Come on, you know you want this." He put one knee on the bed and took hold of the waistband of her jeans. She jerked against the ropes, but even if she hadn't been securely tied, she couldn't have overcome his greater physical strength. She closed her eyes.

With a splintering crash the door flew open. Deputy Hal Knight and his part-time assistant deputy Liz Bergen stood in the hallway, both in rain-streaked, unbuttoned trench coats. They hadn't drawn their weapons, but Hal's hand was on the butt of his. They took in the scene at a glance. Teresa was afraid Frank would grab for the knife, but he took a step back and raised his hands. "Well, this is embarrassing," he said. "To what do we owe this interruption?"

Liz came quickly into the room, threw the bedspread over Teresa, and slipped the handcuffs off her belt. "Move away from the bed, McAllister," she said. "You're under arrest."

"I don't think so," Frank said. "And it's Officer McAllister to you. This is totally consensual. We've been involved for a while now. We're engaged." He zipped his pants and made a move toward his shoes, but Liz made a preemptory gesture to stop him.

Hal Knight cleared his throat. "She asked you to use a knife?"

"It was a rape fantasy," Frank said and added,

spreading his hands, "Hey, don't judge."

Knight looked at Teresa, and she shook her head. She was too overwhelmed to speak and didn't think she needed to. Frank was a police officer, but this was Cougar, and he was new in town. She knew who would be believed. Liz gestured for Frank to turn around and cuffed his hands behind him. He didn't resist. "This is a bogus arrest, and you know it," he said. "Teresa, tell them." He sounded so plausible she almost believed him herself, but a minute ago she had been really scared.

All she could say was, "Will somebody please untie me?" Hal came to the bed and used the tip of his utility knife to tease out the knots on her wrists and slip the ropes off. The serrated blade might have been faster, but it was evidence now. As soon as her hands were free, he took the belt off her neck before he started on her ankles. She tried to hold still, but she was shaking with relief.

"Teresa," Frank said. "Don't hang me out to dry. Tell them." She shook her head. "This isn't like you," he said. Liz picked up his shoes and took his arm. "We'll talk later," he said to Teresa as she led him out.

"Where is Aiden?" she asked anxiously, trying to hold her T-shirt together as Hal helped her off the bed.

"Locked in the bathroom," he said. "Brett Devlin is with him." It must have been one of the deputies, then, not Aiden, who rattled the doorknob, but what was Brett doing here? It didn't make any sense, but the whole night had been surreal.

She could only focus on one thing. "I need to see him."

"As soon as McAllister is out of the way."

"Thank you," she remembered to say. She rubbed her right wrist and showed him the red marks on both of them.

He looked into her eyes, assessing her. "Do you want to press charges?" he asked.

"I guess I have to, don't I? To protect the next woman?"

"Leave the ropes tied on the bed, and don't throw away your shirt." he said. "We'll come back tomorrow with a camera and evidence bags, and take a detailed statement. We don't need to do it tonight. I assume you'd prefer to wait until your son is in school. We'll fix the damage to the door, too." She didn't think the PCPD would have—another advantage of living in a small town. "You probably won't want to sleep in here tonight anyway," Hal said. "We can take you to a hotel or a friend's house if you'd like."

"I want to stay here," she said. "I'll sleep with Aiden." As if she would sleep! "I need to see him," she said again. She couldn't wait any longer and rushed into the hall.

Hal came out right behind her, rapped on the bathroom door, and called, "The coast is clear," and Brett opened it, a hand on her son's shoulder.

"Mama!" Aiden cried and flung himself at her. She held him close and looked up at Brett. He was wearing a comfortable jacket with elbow patches, one she had seen him wear many times. He took it off and held it out to her. She let go of Aiden and put it on gratefully. It was slightly damp but warm, and it smelled like Brett in some indefinable way. It felt familiar and safe, but there were too many people in the small space of the hall, and she was starting to feel crowded.

"I need to sit down," she said. She took Aiden's hand, and the men followed them into the living room. Liz and Frank were gone. She couldn't see anything through the curtains, but flashes of light from the police car filled the window. She sat on the couch, pulled the boy onto her lap, and gave him a fierce hug.

"How did you know?" she asked Hal. He nodded toward Aiden.

"He called 911?" She had taught him how, but was amazed to think he had.

"No," Brett said. "He texted me. I called 911, and I got here the same time they did." She didn't want to think about what might have happened if he had arrived first.

"You texted Brett?" she asked Aiden. She hadn't known he knew the number—maybe Brett had programmed it in when he checked for an app.

Brett held out his phone for her to see. The text read, "Bad man n my house. Mama scaired."

Teresa started to cry. She wasn't sure why. She should have laughed, thinking how embarrassed they would all have been if it *had* been consensual. "You're my hero!" she said tearfully. "But how did you know? Sweetie, how did you know the bad man was in the house?" She was shaking and trying not to. She didn't want to scare him. How could she explain that the bad man was his SWAT hero?

"Door closed," he signed. Hal was a relative stranger to him; he wouldn't use his voice in front of him. "Bad man coat." He pointed to the overcoat on the back of the easy chair, still wet from the rain, a coat he had never seen Frank wear. "Light off." He pointed to the TV, where Marisa Tomei's face was frozen on the screen, and to the bowl of ice cream on the coffee table, melted now to slush. "Ice cream."

For Hal's benefit she said, "My bedroom door was closed, and you saw the coat and that I left the TV on and didn't finish my ice cream?"

"A real little detective," Hal said admiringly.

"I heard you call me after the lightning," Teresa said to Aiden. "Did it scare you?"

"No. I wake up. I look for you in kitchen."

"How did you know I was scared?"

He shrugged. He pointed again to the ice cream. "Can I have?"

Teresa laughed and gave him an affectionate squeeze. "Yes, you can have as much ice cream as you want. You were so brave. I'm so proud of you!" She kissed his forehead.

Liz Bergen had returned and was waiting to talk to her. Brett picked up the melted ice cream and held his hand out to Aiden. "I'll get you your own bowl," he said and took him into the kitchen.

"Are you okay?" Liz asked. "We can take you to the hospital to be checked out."

"I'd rather stay here," she said. "I'm fine, just a little shaky."

"Will we need to do a rape kit?"

"No. You got here just in time."

"Attempted rape and false imprisonment, then," Liz said.

Hal Knight nodded. "Don't touch anything in the bedroom," he said. "We'll be back tomorrow. Are you okay here now?"

"I'm fine. I'll give you my phone, too—the one he gave me. He put something on it."

Both officers were ready to leave. She got up, still a little uncertain on her feet but calmer now. "Thank you both so much," she said. "If Frank—Mr. McAllister—makes bail, will you let me know?"

Liz said, "Yes, of course." She took Frank's overcoat and left.

Hal patted her arm. "It's been quite a week," he said. "A body in the dump, and now this. I must confess, when I saw he had something around your neck…"

An unnatural calm came over Teresa. "Hal? Elle Goodman and the girl from Yaholo—do you think they were killed by the same man?"

"Could be," he said. "We don't have all the facts yet."

"They were strangled? Do you know what with?"

"Not for sure. The investigations are still ongoing. We might never know about the Yaholo victim. She might have been manually strangled, like Linedecker's victims, but Miss Goodman had ligature marks." He was in a familiar, chatty mood now, standing casually with his uniform hat in his hands.

"Do you have any suspects?"

"Nope. Certainly not Linedecker—best alibi in the world. I knew the Yaholo girl wasn't his, even before we were sure her death was too recent. His were both blonde waitresses. Plus Linedecker buried his victims fully clothed, and the gal from Yaholo was practically naked."

"The newspaper report said Elle was partially clad too. Do you know what they were wearing?"

He didn't seem to think the question was odd. "The fabric was too deteriorated to be sure on the first one, but she was nude from the waist down. Miss Goodman was wearing only a brassiere."

Leave your bra on...I just like it that way.

She met Hal's eyes. "Make sure Mr. McAllister has an alibi for Halloween," she said.

He gave her a speculative look, but he said only, "I guess we're through here for tonight," put on his hat, and left.

Brett was standing in the kitchen doorway. She didn't know how long he had been there. He came toward her hesitantly, and then she was in his arms. She fit so perfectly there, her head nestled against his shoulder. She had forgotten how good they were together. She had always felt safe with his arms around her. "I've missed this," he said against her hair. They had been friends for so long, and she had always loved him. He didn't ask about what had happened. He just held her.

"Thank you for being there for Aiden," she said. "Let me get a robe, and I'll give you back your jacket." He let go of her, but followed her into the bedroom. She opened the closet door, and then she saw him staring at the bed, where the ropes were still tied. She gestured toward the belt and indicated her neck. He looked at her, shocked, without words. She was glad he hadn't seen her helpless and vulnerable.

She took off his jacket, put on a warm robe, cinched the belt tight, and stepped into her slippers. "I was so scared," she said abruptly. Brett put his arms around her again. His hand was on her hair. Awkwardly, uncertainly, he kissed her. He had been foolish. She had been foolish. None of it mattered now.

"Mama?" Aiden called from the kitchen.

"Is there any triple chocolate left?" she asked.

"Yeah," Brett said. "Let's go finish it off."

Hands linked, they went to join Aiden in the kitchen. "What are you doing on Thanksgiving?" Teresa asked.

A word about the author...

Linda Griffin retired as Fiction Librarian for the San Diego Public Library to spend more time on her writing, and her work has been published in numerous journals. The Wild Rose Press published her romance *Seventeen Days* in 2018.

In addition to the three Rs—reading, writing, and research—she enjoys Scrabble, movies, and travel.

Find Linda at:

http://www.lindagriffinauthor.com/
http://www.facebook.com/lindagriffin.author
http://www.twitter.com/LindaGriffinA